The
History
of the
World

According to

The History of the World

According to
facebook

Wylie Overstreet (author)

itbooks

AN IMPRINT OF HARPERCOLLINS*PUBLISHERS*

*it***books**

HarperCollins books may be purchased for educational, business, or sales promotional use. For information please write: Special Markets Department, HarperCollins Publishers, 10 East 53rd Street, New York, NY 10022.

FIRST EDITION

Designed by Timothy Shaner, nightanddaydesign.biz

Library of Congress Cataloging-in-Publication Data is available upon request.

ISBN 978-0-06-207618-2

11 12 13 14 15 /QGT 10 9 8 7 6 5 4 3 2 1

For my parents.

Introduction

Ah, Facebook. We all make fun of it, and we're all on it. If the Facebook community—600 million strong—were a country, it would rank third in population and last in spelling ability. Nowadays Facebook is visited more often than Google, presumably because Google isn't as robust of a digital stalking tool.

But Facebook has only been around since 2004. In the grand scheme of things, this is not very long; in the time since, we've seen wars begin and end, revolutions succeed and fail, Lady Gaga wear a dress made of bacon, and this author go from madly in love to dumped and despondent, though he's not bitter. Tali. You bitch.

But the universe has been around for 13 billion years or, if you like reading fantasy novels, 12,000. What if Facebook had been around to record it all on that adorable little news feed? The dawn of time, of life, of man and civilization, of all our fits and starts, wars and squabbles, achievements and failures? What if Galileo was a tagging fiend, if Hitler liked his own statuses, if Patton checked in across North Africa posting pictures to make everyone envy how awesome his summer was going? Historians would probably sigh deeply, pour themselves a double, and mutter something about a "literary perversion" or "no respect for the field," or unrelatedly "where the hell are my goddamn keys."

2 The History
of the World
According to **facebook**

Let's let them drink and look for their belongings and/or a better career while we take a look at the annals of history according to Facebook—from its first moments all those years ago to the present day. I sincerely hope you enjoy this book. You may find it educational, you may find it amusing, or you may find it on the back of a toilet while pooping, in which case you're not going anywhere for a while. Might as well flip through.

Again, enjoy.

And wash your hands.

The Singularity FIRST!!1!
13 billion years ago • Comment • Like

>
>
> **The Singularity** Only one here. Right.
> 13 billion years ago • Like

The Singularity Phenomenal cosmic power, itty-bitty living space.
13 billion years ago • Comment • Like

>
>
> **Genie** wurd.
> 13 billion years ago • Like

The Singularity is in a relationship with **Space** and **Time**, and it's complicated.
 13 billion years ago • Comment • Like

>
>
> **Laws of Physics** Really complicated.
> 13 billion years ago • Like

The Singularity

 Singularity to Host "Big Bang" Cosmic Inauguration
All Matter in Universe **Attending,** Even Creationists

📑 13 billion years ago • Comment • Like

The Big Bang such a great party, thanks for everything that came.
13 billion years ago • Comment • Like

>
>
> **Dark Matter** Just got here! Did I miss it?
> 13 billion years ago • Like

> **The Big Bang** Yeah, sorry. It only lasted 3 trillionths of a second.
> 13 billion years ago • Like

The Universe pics from my birthday party

 13 billion years ago • Comment • Like

👍 **Carl Sagan** likes this.

 The Universe is now married to **Entropy**.
💚 13 billion years ago • Comment • Like

 The Second Law of Thermodynamics Watch out, she'll drain you. Trust me.
13 billion years ago • Like

🌳⬇ **Gravity > Nebula** Ya got talent, kid, I'll give ya that. With my help you could even be famous... be a somebody, ya know? You watch, stick with me kiddo and I'll make ya a star!
13 billion years ago • Comment • Like

👍 **Fusion** likes this.

 The Sun is now friends with **Earth** and 7 other planets.

13 billion years ago • Comment • Like

 Pluto Not cool.
13 billion years ago • Like

Uranus For the last time, the accent is on my FIRST syllable.
13 billion years ago • Comment • Like

Mercury I hear you're full of gas.
13 billion years ago • Like

Jupiter lol
13 billion years ago • Like

God Okey doke, time to make some shit. Starting with the Heavens and Earth.
13 billion years ago • Comment • Like

God Wait, I can't see a thing. I wonder if I can maybe...
13 billion years ago • Like

God Ah! Let there be it!

Light

13 billion years ago • Comment • Like

God tagged the **Heavens** and the **Earth** in his own album.

  The Beginning

13 billion years ago • Comment • Like

Earth is in a domestic partnership with the **Moon**.
💚 13 billion years ago • Comment • Like

👍 **Tides** like this.

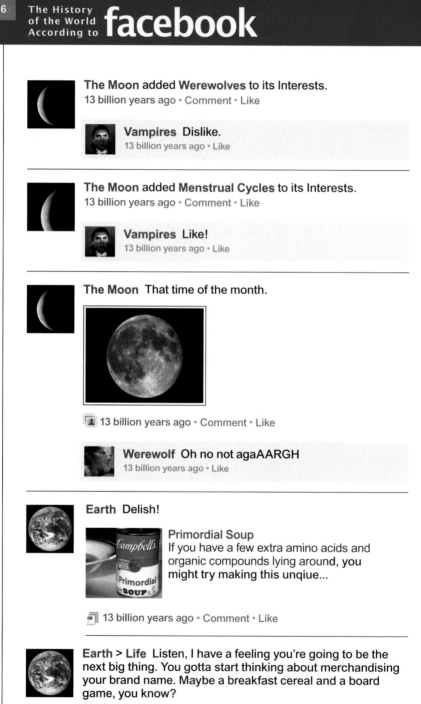

The Moon added **Werewolves** to its Interests.
13 billion years ago • Comment • Like

Vampires Dislike.
13 billion years ago • Like

The Moon added **Menstrual Cycles** to its Interests.
13 billion years ago • Comment • Like

Vampires Like!
13 billion years ago • Like

The Moon That time of the month.

13 billion years ago • Comment • Like

Werewolf Oh no not agaAARGH
13 billion years ago • Like

Earth Delish!

Primordial Soup
If you have a few extra amino acids and organic compounds lying around, you might try making this unqiue...

13 billion years ago • Comment • Like

Earth > Life Listen, I have a feeling you're going to be the next big thing. You gotta start thinking about merchandising your brand name. Maybe a breakfast cereal and a board game, you know?
13 billion years ago • Comment • Like

Single-Celled Organism is in a relationship with itself.
💜 13 billion years ago • Comment • Like

 Earth ??
13 billion years ago • Like

 It's complicated between **Single-Celled Organism** and itself.
💜 13 billion years ago • Comment • Like

 Earth wtf?
13 billion years ago • Like

 Single-Celled Organism is separated from itself.
💜 13 billion years ago • Comment • Like

👍 **Mitosis** likes this.

 Earth Ooooooh. Got it. Nice.
13 billion years ago • Like

 Life is in a relationship with **Evolution**.
💜 13 billion years ago • Comment • Like

 Life added **Photosynthesis** to its Interests.
13 billion years ago • Comment • Like

 The Sun Mooch.
13 billion years ago • Like

 Life Not sure if I can survive on land.
13 billion years ago • Comment • Like

 Dr. Ian Malcolm Pretty sure that, that, uh, you will, uh... find a way.
13 billion years ago • Like

 Evolution I got your back.
13 billion years ago • Like

Life created an event.

Cambrian Explosion
Single-Cell is so last millennium! Come ring in Multi-Cell and get all mutated!

📅 13 billion years ago • Comment • Like • Share • RSVP to this event

Evolution Can't wait. I'm gonna get drunk and go bonkers.
13 billion years ago • Like

Earth is now friends with **Flora** and **Fauna**.

13 billion years ago • Comment • Like

Tyrannosaurus Rex

13 billion years ago • Comment • Like

Stegosaurus Badass pic, Rex. Except what's up with your arms?
13 billion years ago • Like

Evolution My mistake. They seemed to make sense at the time.
13 billion years ago • Like

Velociraptor added **Problem Solving** to its Interests.
13 billion years ago • Comment • Like

Earth Clever girl.
13 billion years ago • Like

Asteroid Hitting up Earth today, if ya know what I mean.
13 billion years ago • Comment • Like

 Tyrannosaurus Rex Noooooooo
13 billion years ago • Like

 Stegosaurus Nooooooooo
13 billion years ago • Like

 Brontosaurus Nooooooooo
13 billion years ago • Like

 Earth fml
13 billion years ago • Like

 Cockroach lol
13 billion years ago • Like

 Mammals > Dinosaurs Na na na naa, hey hey hey... goodbye.

 Dinosaurs Extinct
Warm-Blooded Wombed Furballs
Take Over Planet

13 billion years ago • Comment • Like

 Primates check out my new opposable thumbs

13 billion years ago • Comment • Like

 Lobster Whoa, weird. What do you use them for?
13 billion years ago • Like

 **Primates** All kinds of things: gripping branches, picking out lice, masturbating, etc.
13 billion years ago • Like

10

The History
of the World
According to facebook

 Lobster What is "masturbating"?
13 billion years ago • Like

 Primates The BEST.
13 billion years ago • Like

 Neanderthal Why doesn't the glowing heat orb just STAY in the sky?!
300,000 years ago • Comment • Like

 Homo Erectus ooo, just discovered this!

300,000 years ago • Comment • Like

 Homo Erectus warm warm warm warm!

300,000 years ago • Comment • Like

 Homo Erectus HOT HOT BURN BURN!

300,000 years ago • Comment • Like

Dawn of Man

After brutal eons of natural selection, evolution managed to iron out the wrinkles of a certain branch of apes and produce a hairless smarty-pants upgrade: us.

Modern science has removed all doubt from Mr. Darwin's theory. Our ancestors were primates—with whom we still share DNA—and long ago we came down from the trees, began walking upright, and evolved a higher intelligence. We started making tools and using fire. We began speaking to each other. If something made us angry, we used language to communicate instead of just shrieking loudly like our tree-dwelling ancestors—or the creationists currently reading this.

Emerging from Africa, our species flourished across the continents. We used our smarts to invent the wheel, agriculture, cargo pants, and Bud Light Lime. Our civilizations spread like the wings of chicken held upside down, proving that we were the planet's dominant species and that analogies are not my strong suit.

The evolution of man was not a perfect process (foreskin? really?), but the emergence of man began an epoch of dominance that will continue in perpetuity, or until we fuck it up.

Homo Sapiens Good news! My brain is huge.
300,000 years ago • Comment • Like

Neanderthal And I just saved a ton of money on my car insurance.
300,000 years ago • Like

God Accidentally sneezed on a pile of dust and now there's a naked dude standing in my foyer. You gotta be careful with this omnipotence thing.
300,000 years ago • Comment • Like

Adam
Nice, but kinda lonely — is in **Eden**.
 300,000 years ago • Comment • Like

Adam Anyone know what long-term complications can arise from a missing rib?
300,000 years ago • Comment • Like

God Pipe down, you'll like what I'm making.
300,000 years ago • Like

Adam is now friends with **Eve**.

 300,000 years ago • Comment • Like

Eve likes **Paradise**.
300,000 years ago • Comment • Like

God Who doesn't, amiright?
300,000 years ago • Like

Eve was tagged in **Snake's** photo.

300,000 years ago • Comment • Like

Snake Make you hungry for one?
300,000 years ago • Like

 Eve Yeah, but this bikini bod isn't gonna keep itself thin.
300,000 years ago • Like

 Snake created an event.

 Fruit Tasting!
Organic, locally grown
and sustainably farmed!

 300,000 years ago • Comment • Like • Share • RSVP to this event

 Eve Sorry, I'm on a master cleanse!
300,000 years ago • Like

 Snake This is harder than I thought.
300,000 years ago • Like

 Eve What is?
300,000 years ago • Like

Snake Nothing, forget it.
300,000 years ago • Like

 Snake > Eve

Study Reveals "Knowledge Apple" Benefits
Slimmer Figure, Clear Skin,
Only One Tiny Caveat

300,000 years ago • Comment • Like

 Eve omg rly?!
300,000 years ago • Like

 Snake Who knew, right?
300,000 years ago • Like

 Eve Wait, what's a "caveat"?
300,000 years ago • Like

Snake Uh... 10 calories.
300,000 years ago • Like

 Eve omg really? I guess I could use a snack...
300,000 years ago • Like

 Adam NO STOP
300,000 years ago • Like

 God > Eve Fail.
300,000 years ago • Comment • Like

 Eve was tagged in **God's** album.

 Childbirth

300,000 years ago • Comment • Like

 Adam Ooooo, sucky.
300,000 years ago • Like

 Akhmed Just invented a way to record language.

Cuneiform Script

30,000 BC • Comment • Like

 Nemenhat Whoa. What's it say?
30,000 BC • Like

Akhmed "Steve owes me a goat."
30,000 BC • Like

 Nemenhat That's all? Seems like there should be more.
30,000 BC • Like

 Steve Bullshit, I owe you a chicken.
30,000 BC • Like

 Akhmed It also says "Steve is a cheap bastard."
30,000 BC • Like

 The Ice Age is now friends with **Earth**.

30,000 BC • Comment • Like

👍 **Glaciers** like this.

 Mayans Sure, we may be dying out, but at least we're aren't those poor suckers who have to be around when it hits the fan in the early 21st century.
30,000 BC • Comment • Like

👍 **Roland Emmerich** likes this.

 God As a token of my gratitude, I gave my boy @Noah a 5-day, 4-night cruise on the (very) high seas!
30,000 BC • Comment • Like

 Noah Whaaaat! This is amazing, G! Thanks!
30,000 BC • Like

 God No worries man, you deserve it. Small note--you gotta build the boat.
30,000 BC • Like

 Noah Wait, what?
30,000 BC • Like

 God And you have to take a breeding pair of every animal with you. So you probably should make it big.
30,000 BC • Like

Noah Whoa, hang on, I don't know about this.
30,000 BC • Like

 God Aaaand there's a giant flood coming, so if you don't, you'll die.
30,000 BC • Like

 Noah Dick.
30,000 BC • Like

 God :-D
30,000 BC • Like

 Noah posted a picture.

📷 30,000 BC • Comment • Like

 God Nice!
30,000 BC • Like

 Noah So is the invoice, which is in the mail.
30,000 BC • Like

 Noah — is in the **Ark** with a **Elephants, Turtles, Guinea Pigs,** and a bajillion other animals.
📍 30,000 BC • Comment • Like

 Noah Wow, smells... really great in here.
30,000 BC • Like

 God Sarcasm doesn't get you into heaven.
30,000 BC • Like

 Noah In hindsight putting the pigeons and jaguars together was a bad move. Also, anyone have any extra pigeons by any chance?
30,000 BC • Comment • Like

Noah > God How about letting those waters recede? It's been a couple days....
30,000 BC • Comment • Like

 God Yeah, no prob. Send out a bird or something to look for land. You got any pigeons?
30,000 BC • Like

 Noah Uh, does a dove work?
30,000 BC • Like

 God Yeah, sure, whatever.
30,000 BC • Like

 Dove

30,000 BC • Comment • Like

 Noah Phew.
30,000 BC • Like

 God Nice. When you die you can come hang with me by my infinity pool and drink mai tais. Hollaaaaa.
30,000 BC • Like

 God > Abraham Big A, you still owe me ten bucks from minigolf last week.
1770 BC • Comment • Like

 Abraham I don't get paid till next month.
1770 BC • Like

 God Well then sacrifice your son to me.
1770 BC • Like

 Isaac Uh, Dad? Why the knife?
1770 BC • Like

Abraham Sorry, kiddo. Hold still.
1770 BC • Like

 God WHOA DUDE STOP
1770 BC • Like

 Abraham But...
1770 BC • Like

 God Sarcasm! Just give me cash whenever, sheesh.
1770 BC • Like

 Abraham Oh. Sorry, I can never tell.
1770 BC • Like

 God Really? You think I'm the kind of guy who'd require the sacrifice of a beloved son?
1770 BC • Like

 Jesus Christ ...
1770 BC • Like

 God That was different.
1770 BC • Like

 Isaac I hate u! Worst dad EVER!
1770 BC • Comment • Like

 Abraham Oh relax. Write about it on your livejournal or something.
1770 BC • Like

 Pharaoh Offering a great investment opportunity in a giant tomb construction project. Buy in early, then recruit others to maximize your returns! Message me for details.
1440 BC • Comment • Like

👍 **Ra** likes this.

 Worker Is this a pyramid scheme?
1440 BC • Like

 Pharaoh Interesting you say that...
1440 BC • Like

Moses > Pharaoh Dude. My people. Let them go.
1440 BC • Comment • Like

 God likes this.

 Pharaoh Look, man, I totally get where you're coming from, but honestly good slave labor is hard to find these days. I gotta keep my eye on the bottom line here, especially with these "Pyramid" things in the works sooo yeah, sorry.
1440 BC • Like

 Moses alright we're outta here
1440 BC • Like

 **Pharaoh** is now friends with **Locusts, Frogs,** and **8 other plagues.**

 1440 BC • Comment • Like

 Moses and **The Israelites** like this.

Pharaoh Alright, GTFO
1440 BC • Like

 Moses Outta here. Parting the Red Sea....

1440 BC • Comment • Like

 Egyptian Soldier :-O
1440 BC • Like

Moses ...aaand closing the Red Sea.
1440 BC • Comment • Like

    Egyptian Soldier wtf is this magic
    1440 BC • Like

    Egyptian Soldier oh no here comes the wat
    1440 BC • Like

    The Israelites lol
    1440 BC • Like

    God Sly move, M! Side note--got a pair of stone
    tablets I'd love for you to take a look at. Hit me on
    the cellie.
    1440 BC • Like

Moses > God "Thou shalt not thank me during post-game
interviews"?
1440 BC • Comment • Like

    God What, I find it insincere.
    1440 BC • Like

    Moses We're taking that one off. 10 is a nice round
    number anyway.
    1440 BC • Like

    God Fine.
    1440 BC • Like

Helen of Sparta — is in **Troy**.
📍 1184 BC • Comment • Like

👍 **Paris** likes this.

    Menelaus thought we were wine tasting today, babe
    1184 BC • Like

Helen of Troy changed her current city to **Troy**.
1184 BC • Comment • Like

    Menelaus Did your acct. get hacked babe?
    1184 BC • Like

22 The History
of the World
According to **facebook**

 Paris If that's what they're calling it these days, then yea lol
1184 BC • Like

 Helen of Sparta is in a relationship with **Paris**.
♥ 1184 BC • Comment • Like

 Menelaus That's it, I'm coming after you, pretty boy.
1184 BC • Like

 Paris haha, you and what army?
1184 BC • Like

Agamemnon Mine.
1184 BC • Like

 Paris O_o
1184 BC • Like

King Priam FML
1184 BC • Like

 Agamemnon A thousand should do it.

🖼 1184 BC • Comment • Like

 Achilles > Odysseus Hey man, did I leave my ankle armor in your chariot?
1184 BC • Comment • Like

👍 **Paris** like this.

 Trojan Army Victory! 10 years of siege and we've finally driven off the Gree... whoa. Wait a tick. Did someone misplace a giant wooden horsey thing?
1184 BC • Comment • Like

Odysseus Oh, dang! Yeah, that's ours... must've left it behind by purpose.
1184 BC • Like

 Odysseus Er, by accident. Anyway, it's all yours. Might look good inside the city walls next to like a fountain or a pillar or something. Anywhere inside the city walls, really.
1184 BC • Like

 Trojan Army Wow, thanks fellas.
1184 BC • Like

 Greek Army Oh of course, it's our city.
1184 BC • Like

 Greek Army Er, our pleasure.
1184 BC • Like

 Penelope long and winding roooooload

 Motley Crue "Home Sweet Home"

1184 BC • Comment • Like

 Odysseus On my way!
1184 BC • Like

 Suitors shit.
1184 BC • Like

 Syrens > Odysseus Hey babe, wanna stop by our island? Promise to make it worth your while ;-)
1184 BC • Comment • Like

 Odysseus I want to go to there.
1184 BC • Like

 Syrens Just park your boat on the rocks.
1184 BC • Like

Syrens I mean the beach.
1184 BC • Like

Odysseus My shipmates are cockblocks and refusing to go. My hands are tied. :-(
1184 BC • Like

 Syrens You're the captain, though!
1184 BC • Like

 Odysseus No, I mean my hands are literally tied to the mast. Actually, this may have been my idea.
1184 BC • Like

 Goliath I swear, you have one off day and everybody hates you. I'm going to go sit in the shower until the hot water runs out.
1020 BC • Comment • Like

👍 **David** likes this.

 Jonah is now friends with **The Whale**.

 765 BC • Comment • Like

 Jonah Can't see a thing in here. And it smells like low tide.
765 BC • Like

 Oedipus is in a relationship with **Queen Jocasta**.
💜 492 BC • Comment • Like

👍 **Queen Jocasta** likes this.

 **Creon** She's a bit older, no?
492 BC • Like

 Sappho OMG so happy for you! You guys look great together! And a little alike, actually.
492 BC • Like

 Oracle of Delphi She's your mom, dude.
492 BC • Like

 Creon LOL JER-RY JER-RY JER-RY!
492 BC • Like

Socrates Got stopped and given a ticket for "corrupting the youth."
399 BC · Comment · Like

👍 **Bill** and **Ted** like this.

 Plato Ouch. What's the fine?
399 BC · Like

 Socrates Hm. Not so bad, it just says I have to drink hemlock.
399 BC · Like

 Plato ...
399 BC · Like

 Aristotle ...
399 BC · Like

 Socrates What?
399 BC · Like

 Plato Hemlock is lethal.
399 BC · Like

Socrates This day just keeps getting better.
399 BC · Like

Socrates > Greek Magistrates For what it's worth, you guys gotta come up with a better way to do this. This hemlock stuff tastes like cut grass. Though it seems to work qui
399 BC · Comment · Like

Alexander the Great — is in **Greece** with the **Macedonian Army.**
📍 330 BC · Comment · Like

Alexander the Great — is in **Persia** with the **Macedonian Army.**
📍 330 BC · Comment · Like

Alexander the Great — is in **Egypt** with the **Macedonian Army.**
📍 330 BC · Comment · Like

26

The History
of the World
According to **facebook**

Alexander the Great — is in **Arabia** with the **Macedonian Army.**

📍 330 BC • Comment • Like

Alexander the Great — is in **Mesopotamia** with the **Macedonian Army.**

📍 330 BC • Comment • Like

Alexander the Great — is in **India** with the **Macedonian Army.**

📍 330 BC • Comment • Like

Macedonian Army You know, we could use a break.
330 BC • Like

Marcus Aurelius Coliseum Madness! Fill out your bracket, winner takes all.
172 BC • Comment • Like

Gladiator Am I on the schedule?
172 BC • Like

Marcus Aurelius Yep! You'll be fighting a tiger.
172 BC • Like

Gladiator I'm sorry?
172 BC • Like

Marcus Aurelius A tiger. Orange cat... stripes...
172 BC • Like

Gladiator I know what a tiger is. I would rather not fight one, as they tend to be furry balls of murder.
172 BC • Like

Gladiator tagged **Marcus Aurelius** in his album.

Are You Not Entertained!?

📷 172 BC • Comment • Like

Oracle > Julius Caesar Had a dream with you in it last night and woke up feeling like I should warn you of... something. Having a hard time recalling it though. Something about March... "The Tides of March" maybe? Ring any bells?
44 BC • Comment • Like

Julius Caesar Nope. Let's not hope it's not life or death.
44 BC • Like

Cleopatra added Eyeliner to her Interests.
44 BC • Comment • Like

👍 **Marc Antony** and **Julius Caesar** like this.

Julius Caesar having a few of the fellas over to the palace tonight for a killer party.
44 BC • Comment • Like

Brutus Oh it's gonna be killer alright.
44 BC • Like

Julius Caesar hahah dude don't be creepy.
44 BC • Like

Age of Wonder

As humanity progressed, we began to question things beyond our immediate understanding. Where did we come from? Why are we here? Who exactly let the dogs out? We dipped our toe into the cold, dark waters of the existential, shivered, and found religion.

God became our guiding light in the darkness of the unknown. We found meaning in His words, comfort in His promise, and a great reason to kill each other in His name. Empirical evidence of his existence remains elusive. Luckily, with humans, the absence of fact is rarely a hindrance. Actually it might get you a show on Fox News.

In the Western world, Christianity became the dominant faith. If you're unfamiliar with Christianity, you're either a remarkably sheltered individual or a member of a malicious alien race who found this book among the ruins of our now-conquered civilization, in which case, welcome, congratulations on your new planet, check out the south of France in the spring. It's lovely.

Today, Christianity offers humans the same basic comforts and purpose it did when we first invent—er, discovered it. It's a chance at salvation and eternal bliss in the embrace of a deity who loves you just the way you are. Unless you are gay.

Mary OMFG. I'm pregnant.
0 BC • Comment • Like

 Joseph Uh you're a virgin, babe. I should know lol
0 BC • Like

 God "OMFG" is right!
0 BC • Like

 Joseph Wait...
0 BC • Like

 Joseph Oh not cool.
0 BC • Like

 Holy Ghost lol someone call Maury.
0 BC • Like

 John the Apostle — is at the **Marriage at Cana** with **Jesus** and **11 others.**
📍 30 • Comment • Like

 John the Apostle Crashing wedding with bunch of friends? $0. Watching J pull his water-into-wine party trick? $0. Everyone's reaction? Priceless.
30 • Like

Peter the Apostle John, come meet us out back by the fire pit. Paul is tanked and singing "Your Body Is a Wonderland" to the bridesmaids.
30 • Like

 Jesus > **Peter the Apostle** dude what happened last night?!
30 • Comment • Like

 Peter the Apostle It got a little crazy, man. Put it this way, we should probably ease up on the partying for a while, and we should definitely not go back to that temple for a looong time.
30 • Like

 Jesus invited you to **The Last Supper.**
🗓 30 • Comment • Like

 Peter the Apostle "Last"?
30 • Like

32

The History
of the World
According to **facebook**

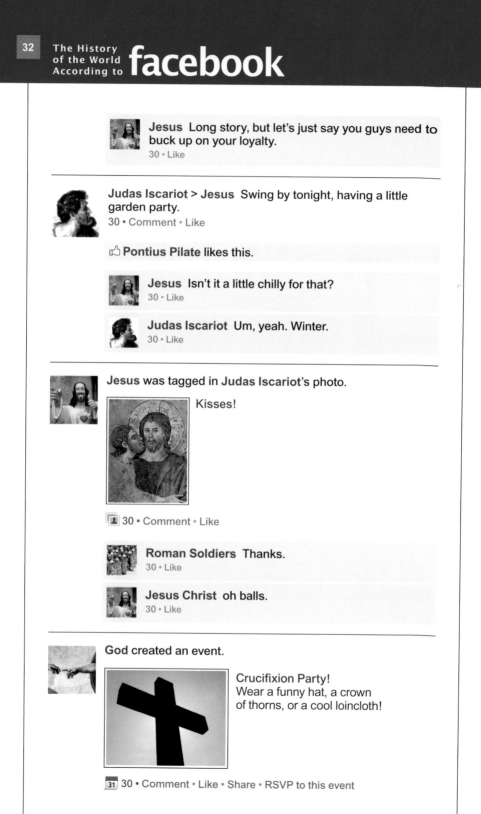

Jesus Long story, but let's just say you guys need to buck up on your loyalty.
30 • Like

Judas Iscariot > Jesus Swing by tonight, having a little garden party.
30 • Comment • Like

👍 **Pontius Pilate** likes this.

Jesus Isn't it a little chilly for that?
30 • Like

Judas Iscariot Um, yeah. Winter.
30 • Like

Jesus was tagged in **Judas Iscariot's** photo.

Kisses!

📷 30 • Comment • Like

Roman Soldiers Thanks.
30 • Like

Jesus Christ oh balls.
30 • Like

God created an event.

Crucifixion Party!
Wear a funny hat, a crown of thorns, or a cool loincloth!

📅 30 • Comment • Like • Share • RSVP to this event

God RSVPed for you, J.
30 • Like

 Jesus You owe me for this.
30 • Like

 Jesus is in The Cave.
📍 30 • Comment • Like

 Peter the Apostle I'm going to come by and pay my respects.
30 • Like

 Jesus Well be quick about it, I'm only here for another 2 days.
30 • Like

 Peter the Apostle wha?!
30 • Like

 Peter the Apostle > Judas Iscariot Dude, what were you thinking?
30 • Comment • Like

👍 **Satan** likes this.

 Judas Iscariot Sorry, but he sayeth-ed unto me one too many times. And whenever I asked him for rent, he'd give me some parable about sowing seeds on stony ground. What does that even mean!? Besides, I owed my cousin Carl thirty pieces of silver.
30 • Like

 Peter the Apostle Wow. So you don't care who his dad is?
30 • Like

 Judas Iscariot His dad?
30 • Like

 Peter the Apostle Starts with a G...
30 • Like

Judas Iscariot Oh fuck.
30 • Like

Zeus > God You gotta let me know how you manage to get heaps of praise and devotion while I'm over here getting offered charred livestock carcasses. These things smell TERRIBLE.
30 • Comment • Like

👍 **Athena** likes this.

Hades Yeah man, it's looking like a damn petting zoo down here with all the new goat souls.
30 • Like

God You gotta have your only child go down there and get crucified.
30 • Like

Jesus Christ Which totally sucks, btw.
30 • Like

God Wonder what this button does....
79 • Comment • Like

Pompeii AHHHHH IT BURNS
79 • Like

God Oh wow. My bad.
79 • Like

Vesuvius LOL
79 • Like

The Dark Ages is friends with **Leprosy**, **Gout**, and **6 other diseases.**

👥 425 • Comment • Like

The Dark Ages Coming to the realization that nothing all that cool happened during my lifetime.
425 • Comment • Like

The Dark Ages There were some pretty gruesome battles I guess. Though that's not exactly all sunshine and rainbows.
590 • Comment • Like

The Dark Ages Oh, and the plague. I had lots of plague. Not fun.
635 • Comment • Like

 Bubonic Plague Whaaat! Dude, we had a blast!
635 • Like

 Peasants A bunch of us starved too.
635 • Like

 The Dark Ages Again, not exactly a good thing.
635 • Like

 The Dark Ages What about the death of the Roman Empire? Does that qualify as important? Still not uplifting, but I'll take important.
770 • Comment • Like

 The Dark Ages In retrospect, my time was just composed of lots of people dying.
810 • Comment • Like

 Industrial Revolution Who are you talking to?
810 • Like

 The Dark Ages Shut up man, you're not even around for another couple centuries.
810 • Like

Renaissance

The Renaissance was a time of profound intellectual, scientific, and artistic growth. After the Dark Ages, centuries over which humanity made great strides in the perfection of starving and dying, the Renaissance was a period of rebirth. It was the age of legendary painters like Leonardo and Raphael as well as sculptors like Michelangelo and Donatello, all of whom valiantly fought the Foot Clan.

Artists were always completing new work, so long as their subject was religious. Scientists were always finding new truths, much to the chagrin of the religious. Yes, the Renaissance gave us innumerable artistic masterpieces, new knowledge about the universe, and many centuries later a type of "Faire" attended by eccentric white folks in costume.

With the exception of Shakespeare, who was OK, I guess, the Renaissance was centered in Italy. We're not sure what they were putting in the water back then, but considering the creative genius it produced, we're hoping Hollywood rips a few lines of it before Adam Sandler has a chance to release another movie.

Renaissance > The Dark Ages Yooo, what up homie! Sorry I'm late, but hey, party doesn't start till I arrrOOH daaaaaamn. What is that smell?! Dude what happened here? This place is a mess.
1045 • Comment • Like

 The Dark Ages -sigh- There was a lot of disease and death.
1045 • Like

 Renaissance I get that, the odors make my eyes water.
1045 • Like

 Ice Age Don't be too hard on yourself, D. All I did was kill things off.
1045 • Like

 Renaissance alright enough with the pity party, who wants to paint a ceiling or invent some shit?
1045 • Like

 The Pope Anyone up for starting a war? Or some witch hunting? Honestly I'm just bored.
1187 • Comment • Like

 Peasant Joe How about an uplifting sermon for your followers?
1187 • Like

 **The Pope** Oh yah that sound great let's do that insteaZZZZzzzzzz. C'mon.
1187 • Like

 The Pope added **Pointy Hats** to his Interests.
1187 • Comment • Like

 The Pope We're out of burning stakes, so I guess I'm conquering the Holy Land.
1187 • Comment • Like

 Muslims Our Holy Land?
1187 • Like

40

The History
of the World
According to **facebook**

 The Pope not for long, lol
1187 • Like

 Muslims Have you ever been here? It's a barren desert.
1187 • Like

 The Pope sure, but it's a HOLY dessert.
1187 • Like

 Muslims Desert.
1187 • Like

 The Pope whatevs
1187 • Like

 Muslim You know that little hat of yours looks awfully a lot like a dunce cap.
1187 • Like

 The Pope What's that?
1187 • Like

 Muslims Wow, is it?
1187 • Like

 The Pope > Richard the Lionheart Broski, this weekend--u, me, ur army, the Holy Land. Boom. Gonna be off the hook.
1187 • Comment • Like

 Richard the Lionheart What Holy Land? Jerusalem?
1187 • Like

 The Pope Yup, and actually it'd just be u, ur army, and the Holy Land. I gotta stay here and do... stuff.
1187 • Like

 Richard the Lionheart Why would we want to conquer a barren desert?
1187 • Like

 The Pope What part of "HOLY" don't u understand?
1187 • Like

The Pope created an event.

 The Crusades
Cuz Their Holy Stuff
Should be Our Holy Stuff

 1187 • Comment • Like • Share • RSVP to this event

 Richard the Lionheart How am I listed as attending? I never responded to this.
1187 • Like

The Pope Made u an admin. U gotta come.
1187 • Like

 Richard the Lionheart changed The Crusades to Pointless Religious Conflict.
 1187 • Comment • Like

The Pope u ASS
1187 • Like

 The Pope changed Pointless Religious Conflict to The Crusades.
1187 • Comment • Like

Richard the Lionheart You know what that hat of yours looks like?
1187 • Like

 Richard the Lionheart — is in **Jerusalem** with **English Crusaders.**
 1187 • Comment • Like

Richard the Lionheart And oh look, it's a barren desert. Shocker.
1187 • Like

The Pope that's it, ur not coming to the afterparty.
1187 • Like

Dante Alighieri Ugh, this is hell.
June 2, 1313 • Comment • Like

 Brunetto Latini Oh no, what is?
June 2, 1313 • Like

 Dante Alighieri This is.
June 2, 1313 • Like

 Brunetto Latini Got that, but what's "hell" right now?
June 2, 1313 • Like

 Dante Alighieri Here. Where I am.
June 2, 1313 • Like

 Brunetto Latini Okaaaay... Where are you?
June 2, 1313 • Like

 Dante Alighieri Hell.
June 2, 1313 • Like

 Brunetto Latini I noticed. Jesus.
June 2, 1313 • Like

 Dante Alighieri You did? Where? I don't think he's down here.
June 2, 1313 • Like

 Brunetto Latini Oh my god. Just tell me where you are.
June 2, 1313 • Like

 Dante Alighieri OK he's *definitely* not around here.
June 2, 1313 • Like

 Brunetto Latini What the hell are you talking about?
June 2, 1313 • Like

 Dante Alighieri Yes! Exactly.
June 2, 1313 • Like

 Brunetto Latini GOD DAMMIT
June 2, 1313 • Like

 Dante Alighieri He did! The whole place!
June 2, 1313 • Like

Satan > **Dante Alighieri** Great times hangin' with you and Virgil, dude. Hope to see you back here soon! Er, not like that.
June 2, 1313 • Comment • Like

👍 **Virgil** likes this.

Robin Hood — is at **Sherwood Forest**.
📍 1400 • Comment • Like

> **Sheriff of Nottingham** CRIMINAL
> 1400 • Like
>
> **Robin Hood** Just trying to spread the wealth around, Sheriff.
> 1400 • Like
>
> **Sheriff of Nottingham** SOCIALIST
> 1400 • Like

Robin Hood is now married to **Maid Marian**.
💜 1400 • Comment • Like

> **Robin Hood** I'd fight for you. I'd lie for you. Walk the wire for you.
> 1400 • Like
>
> **Friar Tuck** Barf.
> 1400 • Like

God > **Joan of Arc** Hey little lady. Just wanted to check in, see what's happening on your farm. From where I sit, I think you should lead the battle to free France.
1430 • Comment • Like

> **Joan of Arc** As you wish, my lord. It shall be my destiny.
> 1430 • Like
>
> **God** Oh wait, my phone autocorrected that. Meant to say "lead the cattle to free grass." Don't go joinin' the war, k?
> 1430 • Like
>
> **God** OK, homegirl?
> 1430 • Like

44 **The History
of the World
According to** facebook

 God Joan? Hello?
1430 • Like

 Joan of Arc is now friends with **Charles VII.**

 1430 • Comment • Like

 Joan of Arc — is at the Siege of Orleans with Charles VII.
 1430 • Comment • Like

👍 **France** likes this.

 God Uh oh.
1430 • Like

Charles VII

 Victory at the Siege of Orleans
Some "Joan" Girl Totally Kicked Ass

1430 • Comment • Like

 God Wow. Not expecting this.
1430 • Like

 Joan of Arc > Charles VII Give me leadership of your entire army.
1430 • Comment • Like

Charles VII Uhhh...why?
1430 • Like

Joan of Arc God told me it was my destiny.
1430 • Like

 God About that...
1430 • Like

Leonardo da Vinci Some new designs.

1430 • Comment • Like

 Hudson Hawk and **Dan Brown** like this.

 Joan of Arc

 Victory at Patay
Joan of Arc Goes 2 for 2,
Signs Endorsement Deal
with Catholic Church

1430 • Comment • Like

 Charles VII GO SHAWTY
1430 • Like

 God Holy crap.
1430 • Like

 Joan of Arc — is in **Reims, France** with **Charles VII**.
1430 • Comment • Like

 Charles VII Holllaaaaa, time to get coronated.
1430 • Like

 God Look, this has been an impressive romp,
but Joan, I really think you gotta ease up before
your luck runs out...
1430 • Like

 English Army Gotcha.
1430 • Like

 God ...like that.
1430 • Like

The History
of the World
According to **facebook**

 Joan of Arc was tagged in **England's** album.

 LOL BBQ

🖼 1430 • Comment • Like

 Joan of Arc I have listened to you, my Lord, and lived my life by your commands.
1430 • Like

 God Mmm... kinda.
1430 • Like

 Joan of Arc What?
1430 • Like

 God Forget it, I'll explain in person. See you in a sec.
1430 • Like

 Christopher Columbus LANDED! Amazing feeling to arrive in... wait does anyone know where we are?
1492 • Comment • Like

 First Mate No idea, sir.
1492 • Like

 Christopher Columbus Anyone care to make an educated guess?
1492 • Like

 Christopher Columbus Anyone? Anyone? Bueller?
1492 • Like

 Francisco Bueller Um... India?
1492 • Like

 Christopher Columbus OK then! India. Hm. Well I guess we'll call these natives "Indians."
1492 • Like

Native Americans Let's hope that doesn't stick.
1492 • Like

 Michelangelo Finished!

August 11, 1503 • Comment • Like

 King David Hey dude, looks great except for one... tiny... thing.
August 11, 1503 • Like

 Michelangelo What? Oooooh, right. Well I was just being true to the original.
August 11, 1503 • Like

 **King David** Alright, wow, not helping. You couldn't have just gone with a fig leaf or a tastefully draped robe?
August 11, 1503 • Like

 Michelangelo I really don't see the problem here.
August 11, 1503 • Like

 Queen Bathsheba Lord knows I do.
August 11, 1503 • Like

 Michelangelo lol
August 11, 1503 • Like

 Leonardo da Vinci added a photo to his album.

 Portrait by an Artist of a Young Woman

1510 • Comment • Like

Mona Lisa What's up with my smile?
1510 • Like

 Leonardo da Vinci 16th-century dentistry, babe. Trust me.
1510 • Like

 Martin Luther Anyone have a hammer I can borrow?
October 31, 1517 • Comment • Like

 Hernan Cortes Just pulled up in the New World. Gonna take a nap, then off to conquer.
March 1519 • Comment • Like

 Aztecs Whoa whoa whoa. This land is occupado, amigo. Also, there's like a hundred of you and a bazillion of us.
March 1519 • Like

 Hernan Cortes You ever meet my friend Smallpox?
March 1519 • Like

 Aztecs Smallwho?
March 1519 • Like

 Hernan Cortes I'll introduce you.
March 1519 • Like

 Henry the VIII Yay great, another daughter. #sarcasm
January 1536 • Comment • Like

 Anne Boleyn Well I can't just will a boy into existence, honey. It's not up to me, so don't lose your head about it.
January 1536 • Like

 Henry the VIII Oh I won't, *honey*. You might.
January 1536 • Like

Michelangelo Done. My arms are sooooooore.

1541 • Comment • Like

 Raphael I'm happy for you, and I'ma let you finish, but Leonardo had one of the best frescos of all time. Of all time.
1541 • Like

 Adam Wow, looks great except you apparently mistook my penis for an infant's.
1541 • Like

 King David I feel ya, man.
1541 • Like

 Copernicus Just discovered that the Earth actually revolves around the Sun.
1543 • Comment • Like

 The Catholic Church hahahahah good one, but we're the center of the universe, bro.
1543 • Like

 Copernicus No, we aren't.
1543 • Like

 The Catholic Church wat
1543 • Like

 Copernicus Would you like to see proof?
1543 • Like

 The Catholic Church SHUT YOUR MOUTH.
1543 • Like

 Romeo Montague So excited for tonight. Want to see my special someone. ;-)
1594 • Comment • Like

Juliet Capulet Me too, babe. I can't wait. <3 <3
1594 • Like

Romeo Montague Oh babe you're so amazing. luv u <3
1594 • Like

Juliet Capulet No you are amazing!!!1! luv u more
1594 • Like

Romeo Montague No luv u more!
1594 • Like

Mercutio Barf.
1594 • Like

Juliet Capulet was tagged in **Romeo Montague**'s album.

Yonder Window Uploads

1594 • Comment • Like

 Juliet Capulet likes this.

Nurse Capulet The creepy guy watching you from the bushes is the one you want to marry?
1594 • Like

Queen Elizabeth added **Celibacy** to her Interests.
1594 • Comment • Like

John Smith Hellooo New World — at **Jamestown, Virginia** with **hundreds of colonists**.
1607 • Comment • Like

Pocahontas changed her hometown from **Just Around the Riverbend** to **Jamestown, Virginia**.
1607 · Comment · Like

 Galileo My new baby.

1609 · Comment · Like

 The Catholic Church wtf is that for? Whatever it is, I don't like it.
1609 · Like

 Galileo It's for keeping your head in the sand.
1609 · Like

 The Catholic Church Oh, really? Huh. That's cool I guess.
1609 · Like

 Pocahontas likes **The Colors of the Wind**.
👍 1614 · Comment · Like

 Church of England > Puritans Friends, Citizens, Countrymen, thou must cease thine Puritan ways and adhere to our religion.
September 6, 1620 · Comment · Like

 Puritans Forsooth, do not let these matters concern you thus, as we shall depart for fairer lands.
September 6, 1620 · Like

 Church of England Doth my ears deceive me? Depart?
September 6, 1620 · Like

52

The History
of the World
According to **facebook**

 Puritans 'Tis true, we hath decided to take our peoples to the New World forthwith.
September 6, 1620 • Like

 Church of England Thou fleest o'er the Atlantic? But why?
September 6, 1620 • Like

 Puritans To be fair, because thou art a dick to us. We seek freedom of faith.
September 6, 1620 • Like

 Church of England Thou ally thyself with a shitty religion.
September 6, 1620 • Like

 Puritans And better ways of spelling "colour" and "favourite."
September 6, 1620 • Like

 Church of England Thou art a bunch of retards.
September 6, 1620 • Like

 Puritans And decent dentistry.
September 6, 1620 • Like

 Church of England Thou knowest what? Thou can go fuck thyself. Go board thy Gayflower already.
September 6, 1620 • Like

 Puritans Mayflower.
September 6, 1620 • Like

 Church of England Whatever.
September 6, 1620 • Like

 Puritans are now friends with **The Atlantic Ocean** and **Boredom**.

September 6, 1620 • Comment • Like

Puritans We hath arrived! Um... somewhere.

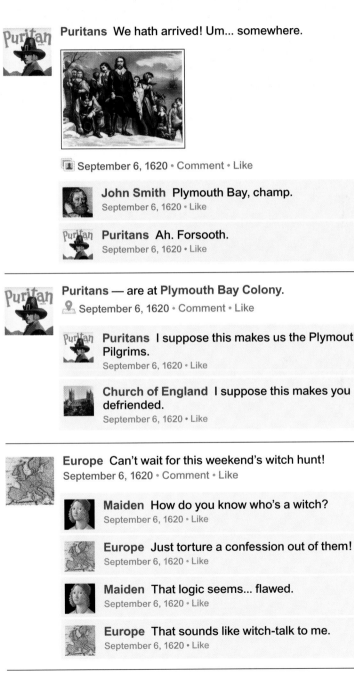

September 6, 1620 • Comment • Like

> **John Smith** Plymouth Bay, champ.
> September 6, 1620 • Like

> **Puritans** Ah. Forsooth.
> September 6, 1620 • Like

Puritans — are at **Plymouth Bay Colony.**

September 6, 1620 • Comment • Like

> **Puritans** I suppose this makes us the Plymouth Pilgrims.
> September 6, 1620 • Like

> **Church of England** I suppose this makes you defriended.
> September 6, 1620 • Like

Europe Can't wait for this weekend's witch hunt!

September 6, 1620 • Comment • Like

> **Maiden** How do you know who's a witch?
> September 6, 1620 • Like

> **Europe** Just torture a confession out of them!
> September 6, 1620 • Like

> **Maiden** That logic seems... flawed.
> September 6, 1620 • Like

> **Europe** That sounds like witch-talk to me.
> September 6, 1620 • Like

Plymouth Pilgrims like Buckles.

👍 September 6, 1620 • Comment • Like

 Plymouth Pilgrims This colonizing thing is harder than it looks. Anyone know how to, like, grow food?

1621 • Comment • Like

> **Native Americans** -sigh- ...give me a shovel, let me show you. And take off that stupid hat.
> 1621 • Like

 Native Americans This does not bode well.

 Helped by Natives, Pilgrims Survive Winter
Colonists Briefly Grateful, Soon Return to Expanding Territory

🗐 1621 • Comment • Like

 Plymouth Pilgrims > Native Americans Guys, wanted to show our gratitude for helping us, you know, not die this past winter by throwing you a big potluck dinner. Whaddya say? Maybe this Thursday?

1621 • Comment • Like

> **Native Americans** Sure! Anything we can bring?
> 1621 • Like

> **Plymouth Pilgrims** Actually, yeah... maybe all the food? We're still not so good at this farming thing.
> 1621 • Like

> **Native Americans.** Oh. Uh, sure. OK.
> 1621 • Like

> **Plymouth Pilgrims** Fab! We'll bring gratitude. And imperialism. And foreign diseases.
> 1621 • Like

> **Native Americans** What?
> 1621 • Like

Plymouth Pilgrims LOL totally kidding!
1621 · Like

 Plymouth Pilgrims Kind of.
1621 · Like

 Galileo Copernicus was right!

 Galileo Proves Heliocentrism
Vein Bulges on Church's Forehead

1632 · Comment · Like

👍 **Logic** and **Reason** like this.

The Catholic Church You're going to regret this.
1632 · Like

 Roman Inquisition > Galileo We need to have a little chat.
1632 · Comment · Like

 Galileo At home. Will be here for a while.
1632 · Comment · Like

The Catholic Church ;-)
1632 · Like

 New England is friends with **New York**, **Boston**, and **8 other cities**.

 1653 · Comment · Like

England Keep it together over there, guys.

 Various Obnoxious Accents Forming in New England Colonies
Broad A, Nasal Tones Catching On

1680 • Comment • Like

 Giacomo Casanova is now friends with **Lady Mercado** and **4 other women. In one night.**

1745 • Comment • Like

 Don Juan NICE.
1745 • Like

 Boston created an event.

 Tea Party!
Protest unfair taxation by making the whole town smell like chamomile!

31 December 16, 1773 • Comment • Like • Share • RSVP to this event

Benjamin Franklin A righteous cause! Let's hope that in the future this event isn't misappropriated by ignorant, angry white people to advocate a backwards political agenda!
December 16, 1773 • Like

 The 13 Colonies are in a relationship with **King George III**, and it's complicated.
♥ 1776 • Comment • Like

King George III WHAT???? Are u serious?
1776 • Like

The 13 Colonies Don't make this harder than it already is. The relationship was long distance and too taxing.
1776 • Like

 King George III So this IS about that whole "no representation" thing. Whatever. Taxes shmaxes.
1776 • Like

 Thomas Jefferson If that's how you feel, then colonies shmolonies...
1776 • Like

 King George III Wait, no, don't!
1776 • Like

 The 13 Colonies are Single.
♥ 1776 • Comment • Like

👍 **Life, Liberty, and The Pursuit of Happiness** like this.

 King George III dammit.
1776 • Like

 Thomas Jefferson Booyah.
1776 • Like

 Ben Franklin lol
1776 • Like

 Ben Franklin tagged **Thomas Jefferson** and **12 others** in a photo.

1776 • Comment • Like

 The United States "The 13 Colonies" never rolled off the tongue.
1776 • Like

John Hancock We have GOT to do this signing thing more often. Such a blast!
1776 • Like

 Thomas Jefferson We noticed.
1776 • Like

 King George III created an event.

 The American Revolutionary War
Because It's Pronounced "to-MAH-to"

31 1776 • Comment • Like • Share • RSVP to this event

 The United States Don't forget to bring your cute wigs.
1776 • Like

 France lol I got your back, America.
1776 • Like

 Paul Revere Waaaaakeuppppptheeeeyy'rehhhheeeerrrreee
1776 • Comment • Like

👍 **Sarah Palin** likes this.

 Marie Antoinette Back from a day of shopping! OMG totally excited about my new summer outfits. Big girly squeeaaaal!
1776 • Comment • Like

 French Peasantry Hey, if you're shopping, mind picking up some bread? We're all out.
1776 • Like

 Marie Antoinette Sorry, I'm on a diet--no carbs. Or favors for poor people. Have cake instead.
1776 • Like

Ludwig van Beethoven

Fur Elise
For a girl i know <3

1776 • Comment • Like

Elise von Rohrenbach "Just friends" means just friends, Ludwig.
1776 • Like

Ludwig van Beethoven >:-(
1776 • Like

Marie Antoinette added **Ignorance** to her Interests.
1776 • Comment • Like

Marie Antoinette I honestly don't even know what that word means!
1776 • Like

The United States > British Army Don't let that screen door hit you on the way out.
1783 • Comment • Like

Wolfgang Amadeus Mozart > Beethoven Great symphony man, really liked it. I wrote one just like it once. When I was six.
1783 • Comment • Like

Ludwig van Beethoven >:-(
1783 • Like

French Peasantry

Revolution in France!
Poor Revolt Against Exploitation
by Rich, Can't Really Blame Them

August 18, 1792 • Comment • Like

60   The History
of the World
According to   facebook

👍 **Democracy** likes this.

 Marie Antoinette Is this like a masquerade ball or something?
August 18, 1792 • Like

 French Peasantry Not quite. It's a party where we'll introduce you to the Guillotine.
August 18, 1792 • Like

 Marie Antoinette Ooo, Guillotine? Is he like a new designer?
August 18, 1792 • Like

 Marie Antoinette is listed as separated from **Her Head**.
💜 August 18, 1792 • Comment • Like

 The French Army has discovered the Rosetta Stone.

📷 1799 • Comment • Like

 Dr. Watson This is astonishing. Have you translated it yet?
1799 • Like

 Professor Picard I have. It's this strange, rambling tale about an unlikable teenage girl who starts at a new high school, completely falls for this creepy kid in her class with pale sparkly skin who fixates on her and her "smell," but it turns out he's a vampire. She's not afraid of him, so they fall in love but, for shockingly unrealistic reasons, never have sex.
1799 • Like

 Dr. Watson Lame.
1799 • Like

Professor Picard Yep.
1799 • Like

 The United States > Meriwether Lewis This weekend, dude. ROAD TRIP. U down!?
1804 • Comment • Like

 Meriwether Lewis Woo! Sure, where to?
1804 • Like

 The United States Dunno!
1804 • Like

 Meriwether Lewis Atlantic City maybe?
1804 • Like

 The United States No no, like literally "I don't know" because it's never been explored.
1804 • Like

 Meriwether Lewis Wha?
1804 • Like

 The United States Well it's not so much a road trip as it is a two-year expedition into the unknown. In fact I'm preeeeeetty certain you won't encounter a single road the entire time.
1804 • Like

 Meriwether Lewis Uh...
1804 • Like

 The United States You leave Tuesday. Buy some oxen and a boat or whatever, and bring that Clark friend of yours.
1804 • Like

William Clark Fuuuuuuuuuu
1804 • Like

 Napoleon Bonaparte Victory. An extra ration of wine for my fine soldiers.
1804 • Comment • Like

Soldier Nice! Always looking out for the little guy.
1804 • Like

Napoleon Bonaparte "Little"?
1804 · Like

 Napoleon Bonaparte What do you mean, "little"? Like midget little? Like I amuse you?
1804 · Like

 Soldier No no! I just... oh god.
1804 · Like

 Napoleon Bonaparte I'm kidding, dude. Go get drunk and name-drop at the parties.
1804 · Like

 Napoleon Bonaparte Invading Asia.
1804 · Comment · Like

 General Sir, I think you're falling victim to one of the classic blunders.
1804 · Like

 Napoleon Bonaparte What? Going against a Sicilian when death is on the line?
1804 · Like

 General No, the other one.
1804 · Like

 Napoleon Bonaparte Pff. Russia is lovely in winter.
1804 · Like

 Nietzsche > God Whoa, I thought you were dead.
1810 · Comment · Like

 Joan Osborne And I was wondering if you're one of us.
1810 · Like

 God Like, a stranger on a bus or something?
1810 · Like

 Joan Osborne Yeah, actually.
1810 · Like

Ludwig van Beethoven WOULD EVERYONE KINDLY SPEAK UP
1820 • Comment • Like

 Andrew Jackson signed the **Indian Removal Act**.
1830 • Comment • Like

 Native American not cool
1830 • Like

 Andrew Jackson Unless ur white
1830 • Like

 The U.S. Treasury tagged **Andrew Jackson** in a photo.

1830 • Comment • Like

👍 **Andrew Jackson** likes this.

 Native American — is on **The Trail of Tears**.
📍 1830 • Comment • Like

 Andrew Jackson kthxbai
1830 • Like

 Andrew Jackson and **Aaron Burr** added **Duels** to their Interests.
1830 • Comment • Like

 Aaron Burr This is what happens when you insult my honor.
1830 • Like

 Alexander Hamilton What honor?
1830 • Like

64

The History
of the World
According to **facebook**

Thomas Jefferson lol
1830 · Like

The Alamo Can't say I'm confident about these odds.
1836 · Comment · Like

> **General Santa Anna** Looks good from where I'm standing.
> 1836 · Like

Davy Crockett GET SOME

🖼 1836 · Comment · Like

👍 **Texas** likes this.

Texas Remember the Alamo!
1836 · Comment · Like

👍 **Jingoism** likes this.

> **Denzel Washington** And the Titans!
> 1836 · Like

> **Earth Wind and Fire** And the 21st niiiiiiight of Septembah!
> 1836 · Like

Charles Darwin added **Theory of Evolution** to his Interests.
1838 · Comment · Like

👍 **Alfred Russel Wallace** and **Thomas Huxley** like this.

> **The Pope** Evowhat?
> 1838 · Like

> **Charles Darwin** This could get awkward.
> 1838 · Like

Charles Darwin Call me crazy, but it appears that all living organisms have evolved from more basic forms over the millenia.
1838 • Comment • Like

 The Catholic Church Hahaha, yeah bro ur crazy.
1838 • Like

 Charles Darwin No, seriously. This is backed by observable evidence.
1838 • Like

 The Catholic Church Lol alright crazy man, that's enough.
1838 • Like

 Charles Darwin In fact, I think it's very likely humans have evolved from primates.
1838 • Like

 The Catholic Church SHUT YOUR FACE. SHUT IT RIGHT NOW.
1838 • Like

 Samuel Morse Invented new communication technology -STOP- Very excited, calling it the "Telegraph" -STOP- Give my love to Mother -STOP-
May 24, 1844 • Comment • Like

 Elizabeth Donner Well great. The pass is closed for the winter, so we're just gonna have to wait this one out. Should be fine, just wish we had brought a little more food.
1846 • Comment • Like

 Elizabeth Donner OK maybe a lot more food.
1846 • Like

 James Donner > Elizabeth Donner I am so OVER this. All the snow, the starvation, the dying, the whole expedition. I'm sick of it. Stick a fork in me, I'm done.
1847 • Comment • Like

 Elizabeth Donner ...
1847 • Like

 James Donner Not like that.
1847 • Like

James Marshall Working up at the lumber mill. Another day, another dollar. Literally.
1849 • Comment • Like

 James Marshall What in the dandy hornswaggle? I do believe I've struck gold!
1849 • Like

 Sneaky Pete Balderdash! Daguerreotype or it didn't happen!
1849 • Like

 James Marshall

🖼 1849 • Comment • Like

 Sneaky Pete By Jove you're right!
1849 • Like

 James Marshall We could make a hundred dollars!
1849 • Like

 Sneaky Pete A hundred dollars? A hundred dollars isn't cool. You know what's cool? A *thousand* dollars.
1849 • Like

 James Marshall HOLY SHIT, GOLD GET YOUR ASSES TO CALIFORNIA, PEOPLE
1849 • Comment • Like

 80,000 people changed their current city to **San Francisco, California.**
1849 • Comment • Like

Charles Darwin Published!

The Origin of Species,
By Means of Natural Selection
Backed Up by Oodles of Scientific
Evidence and Fossil Records

1850 • Comment • Like

The World Whooaaaa.
1850 • Like

The Catholic Church SON OF A BITCH
1850 • Like

The United States

Citing Allergy to Excitement, America
Adopts Baseball as National Pastime

1856 • Comment • Like

👍 **Peanuts** and **Crackerjacks** like this.

The Home Team We didn't win.
1856 • Like

The United States Shame.
1856 • Like

Abraham Lincoln signed the **Emancipation Proclamation**.
January 1, 1863 • Comment • Like

Plantation Owner wtf!? u can't just take away a
man's rights like that! U treatin' us like animals!
January 1, 1863 • Like

Slave Please take a step back and read what you
just wrote.
January 1, 1863 • Like

Plantation Owner hey, did I say u could talk?
January 1, 1863 • Like

 Slave The hypocrisy here is just astounding.
January 1, 1863 • Like

 Plantation Owner Hypowhat? Is that slave talk or somethin'?
January 1, 1863 • Like

 Cornelius Vanderbilt NBD.

 Vanderbilt Buys Saturn
Railroad Tycoon Declares Planet's Rings Will "Look Swell" on Mantel

January 1, 1863 • Comment • Like

 Abraham Lincoln — is in **Gettysburg, Pennsylvania** with the **Union Army**.
November 19, 1863 • Comment • Like

 Abraham Lincoln You bring the speech?
November 19, 1863 • Like

 Speechwriter Uh, I thought you had it.
November 19, 1863 • Like

 Abraham Lincoln You gotta be kidding me.
November 19, 1863 • Like

 Speechwriter I'm sorry, sir. I don't have it.
November 19, 1863 • Like

Abraham Lincoln I can't... We'll do it live.
November 19, 1863 • Like

Speechwriter OK.... um...
November 19, 1863 • Like

 Abraham Lincoln WE'LL DO IT LIVE. FUCK IT. I'LL WRITE IT, AND WE'LL DO IT LIVE.
November 19, 1863 • Like

Abraham Lincoln likes **Stove Pipe Hats** and **Not Smiling.**

👍 April 9, 1865 • Comment • Like

Robert E. Lee — is at **Appomattox** with **Ulysses S. Grant.**

📍 April 9, 1865 • Comment • Like

 Ulysses S. Grant Sooo we're cool, right?
April 9, 1865 • Like

 Robert E. Lee Yeeah... we're cool.
April 9, 1865 • Like

 Ulysses S. Grant You boys promise not to hold a grudge?
April 9, 1865 • Like

 Robert E. Lee Promise.
April 9, 1865 • Like

 Ulysses S. Grant Promise your descendants won't fly Confederate flags from their pickup trucks as a sign of "Southern pride" even though it's the banner of slavery?
April 9, 1865 • Like

 Robert E. Lee One step at a time.
April 9, 1865 • Like

The Union is now friends with **Georgia**, **Virginia**, and **9 other states.**

👥 April 9, 1865 • Comment • Like

👍 **The United States** likes this.

Abraham Lincoln Going to the theater tonight with the missus... got private box seats, baby!
April 14, 1865 • Comment • Like

👍 **John Wilkes Booth** likes this.

Industrial Revolution

Advancements in machinery allowed manufacturing, transportation, and agriculture to boom, triggering a level of socioeconomic growth that the world had never seen. Factories sprung up, the steam engine gained steam, and people ceased their agrarian toil and flocked to cities to begin their first "9 to 5"—though admittedly it was less "9 to 5" and more "9 to Sleep at Your Loom, Woman."

A 140-hour workweek wasn't without its perks, however: free bandages for bleeding fingers, sick leave for the dead, a 15-minute break for pregnant women to perform a standing birth, and prior to their first shift newborns were allowed to dry. It was the best of times, it was the worst of times. Mostly the worst of times.

Through hardship nations prospered. England grew rich off its export of textiles, iron, sooty-faced orphans, and depressing literature. America pushed westward with its railways and became the world's premier tobacco supplier, kicking off a pretty illustrious career helping folks die.

The Industrial Revolution was the first step in modernization, and the world has never looked back. Except on *Antiques Roadshow,* only on PBS.

Union Pacific Railroad — is at **Promontory, Utah** with **Central Pacific Railroad**.

📍 1868 • Comment • Like

 Leland Stanford With that done, I'm off to found a university.

 Transcontinental Railroad Complete! Industrialist Leland Stanford Joins Railways with Blingin' Gold Spike

📑 1868 • Comment • Like

 Union Pacific Railroad Here's to the next century of rail travel!
1868 • Like

 Henry Ford heh heh
1868 • Like

 Alexander Graham Bell Can you hear me now?
1874 • Comment • Like

 General Custer — is at **Little Big Horn** with the **7th Cavalry Regiment**.

📍 June 25, 1876 • Comment • Like

 General Custer Chased off some savages, all is quiet at Little Big Horn.
June 25, 1876 • Like

 General Custer Boy, it's really quiet.
June 25, 1876 • Like

 General Custer Like, too quiet.
June 25, 1876 • Like

New York Times

Motion Picturegraph Show Wows Audiences
"Amazing" Two-Second Loop of Horse Running; "Man Doing Somersaults" Sequel Planned

June 19, 1878 • Comment • Like

👍 **Eadweard Muybridge** likes this.

Hollywood, California I have a great idea.
June 19, 1878 • Like

Thomas Edison Just had a *bright* idea!

October 22, 1879 • Comment • Like

> **Nikola Tesla** If only your puns were as good as your inventions.
> October 22, 1879 • Like

> **Thomas Edison** You're just jealous because you don't *shine* like me.
> October 22, 1879 • Like

> **Nikola Tesla** Stop.
> October 22, 1879 • Like

John Pemberton Threw some ingredients together to make a little tonic. Some carbonated water, a bunch of sugar, some cola nut. Anyone want to try?
October 22, 1879 • Comment • Like

> **Lab Technician** It's tasty, but it's missing... something...
> October 22, 1879 • Like

John Pemberton Just added a bunch of coca leaf extract. Try that.
October 22, 1879 • Like

 Lab Technician OkWOWmuchbetterIfeelgreat.
October 22, 1879 • Like

 Marty McFly Where the hell am I now WHOA INDIANS

 September 5, 1885 • Comment • Like

 Indians WHOA METAL DEMON
September 5, 1885 • Like

 Helen Keller slkef n2 0Dd cn vsdlk3 lkjdf.
June 15, 1890 • Comment • Like

 Annie Sullivan This is going be tough.
June 15, 1890 • Like

 The United States

 President William McKinley Assassinated
Nation Mourns Death

 September 6, 1901 • Comment • Like

The United States He will never be forgotten.
September 6, 1901 • Like

The United States For a little while, at least.
September 6, 1901 • Like

76   The History
of the World
According to facebook

 The United States I mean, let's be honest, 110 years from now, say "William McKinley" to most Americans and you'll be met with blank stares.
September 6, 1901 • Like

 The United States I don't mean to be insensitive, of course. But I just see some future wiseass writer trying to make a joke about the whole assassination, and yet nobody knows who this McKinley guy was! The writer would have to make a big, wordy production to explain the joke, it'd undoubtedly fail, and he'd just have to apologize for even writing such lousy stuff.
September 6, 1901 • Like

 The United States btw I'm sorry.
September 6, 1901 • Like

 Picasso added **The Color Blue** and **Nudes** to his Interests.
February 2, 1902 • Comment • Like

 Railroad > Ocean Liners party's over, bro.

 Wright Brothers Create Aeroplane Machine
Nation, Birds "Astonished to See Man Fly"

 December 17, 1903 • Comment • Like

Zeppelin Impractical.
December 17, 1903 • Like

 Humpty Dumpty Great view from where I'm sitting.
April 11, 1904 • Comment • Like

Humpty Dumpty OH SHI
April 11, 1904 • Like

 Humpty Dumpty > King's Horses Fellas, a little help?
April 11, 1904 • Comment • Like

King's Horses Sorry, man, we did our best.
April 11, 1904 • Like

 King's Men Ditto.
April 11, 1904 • Like

 Humpty Dumpty -sigh-
April 11, 1904 • Like

 King's Men's Sooooooo... omelets then?
April 11, 1904 • Like

 San Francisco Giant earthquake just rolled through, and now fires are raging all over the place.

April 18, 1906 • Comment • Like

 Oscar Wilde You'll be flaming long after the fires go out, honey.
April 18, 1906 • Like

 San Andreas Fault Sorry. That's my fault... er, my fault's fault. You get what I'm saying.
April 18, 1906 • Like

 Picasso added **Cubes** to his Interests.
April 18, 1906 • Comment • Like

 Henry Ford

 Ford Motor Company Unveils "Automobile" Machine
Carriage Makers Go Home, Kick Dog, Quietly Weep

September 27, 1908 • Comment • Like

Ford Model T > Horse Sorry, man. I feel bad about this.
September 27, 1908 • Comment • Like

Horse Why? I don't have to work anymore.
September 27, 1908 • Like

Ford Model T Oh. Huh. How are you gonna spend your time now?
September 27, 1908 • Like

Horse I dunno. I'll chill in pastures. Be an object of affection for young girls. Be an object of desire for women who like to braid hair. Graze. Maybe show up in a parade, do some pooping. Whatevs.
September 27, 1908 • Like

Chicago Cubs And it won't be long before we win another. hollaaaa

Chicago Cubs Win!
1908 World Series Champions

October 14, 1908 • Comment • Like

Theodore Roosevelt Presidency done. Off to shoot an elephant, and/or anything else that moves. Laterzzz.
March 25, 1909 • Comment • Like

R.M.S. Titanic Here's to a flawless maiden voyage.
April 14, 1912 • Comment • Like

👍 **Hubris** and **Fate** like this.

R.M.S. Titanic > Security Little help--crazy dude at the bow yelling about how he's the king of the world.
April 14, 1912 • Comment • Like

Security We're on it.
April 14, 1912 • Like

R.M.S. Titanic > Iceberg Out of the way, fella.
April 14, 1912 • Comment • Like

> **Iceberg** I can't move for you, sir.
> April 14, 1912 • Like

> **Titanic** It's like that?
> April 14, 1912 • Like

> **Iceberg** No, I literally cannot move on my own accord. I'm an iceberg.
> April 14, 1912 • Like

 R.M.S. Titanic Bonked an iceberg, no big deal tho when you're UNSINKABLE.
April 14, 1912 • Comment • Like

> **Iceberg** You sure?
> April 14, 1912 • Like

> **Titanic** Yeah. Why?
> April 14, 1912 • Like

> **Iceberg** Give it a second.
> April 14, 1912 • Like

> **Titanic** ...??
> April 14, 1912 • Like

> **Titanic** You son of a bitch.
> April 14, 1912 • Like

> **Titanic String Quartet** You want us to stop playing?
> April 14, 1912 • Like

> **Titanic** Nope. You're coming with me.
> April 14, 1912 • Like

New York Times

 Titanic Sinks!
Lost to the Depths: 1,517 Souls, Blossoming Love Between Rich Girl and Poor Boy

April 14, 1912 • Comment • Like

Titanic checked in to the **Ocean Floor.**
April 14, 1912 • Comment • Like

👍 **James Cameron** likes this.

Germany, Britain, and 4 other European Powers like **Nationalism** and **Imperialism.**
👍 1913 • Comment • Like

The United States Eaaaasy, fellas.
1913 • Like

Archduke Franz Ferdinand up late working on uniting the empire, and trying to figure out if my mustache can get any more awesome. Boioioioing!
June 28, 1914 • Comment • Like

Archduke Franz Ferdinand checked in to **Sarajevo.**
June 28, 1914 • Comment • Like

Gavrilo Princip > Archduke Franz Ferdinand Taste lead, TYRANT!
June 28, 1914 • Comment • Like

Serbia > Gavrilo Princip why why WHY did you do that!?!!?!!?!!
June 28, 1914 • Comment • Like

Gavrilo Princip Oh c'mon, he was an oppressor. What's the worst that can happen?
June 28, 1914 • Like

Austria-Hungary

Austria-Hungary Declares War on Serbia
World Winces: "This Might Snowball"

June 28, 1914 • Comment • Like

Gavrilo Princip Oh.
June 28, 1914 • Like

 Serbia Yeah.
June 28, 1914 • Like

 Germany is in a domestic partnership with **Austria-Hungary**.
♥ June 28, 1914 • Comment • Like

 Germany > Russia We're at war!
August 1914 • Comment • Like

 Germany > France We're at war!
August 1914 • Comment • Like

 Belgium > Germany We're at war!
August 1914 • Comment • Like

 Britain > Germany We're at war!
August 1914 • Comment • Like

 France > Britain We're at... wait, no, sorry.
August 1914 • Comment • Like

 France > Austria-Hungary We're at war!
August 1914 • Comment • Like

 Britain > Austria-Hungary We're at war!
August 1914 • Comment • Like

Germany > Russia We're at war!
August 1914 • Comment • Like

 Russia Already sent that to me.
August 1914 • Like

 Germany oh right.
August 1914 • Like

 Germany > United States We're at war!
August 1914 • Comment • Like

 United States Is someone writing all this down?
August 1914 • Like

 Germany That's a good idea actually.
August 1914 • Like

 The London Star Tribune Herald Sentinel Ledger Times

Everyone Declares War on Everyone Else
No, Really: Literally Everyone Is All Up in This Shit

August 1914 • Comment • Like

 France, Britain, and **Germany** like Trenches.
👍 August 1914 • Comment • Like

 French Soldiers added **Dying** to their Interests.
August 1914 • Comment • Like

👍 **German Soldiers** like this.

 Britain Jolly good day! Gained 18 feet on the front, only
34,000 dead.
September 12, 1918 • Comment • Like

👍 **Attrition** likes this.

France Hey, not bad! Gained 14 inches, lost 8,000.
Oh wait.... carry the 1... no, that should be 80,000.
Not great, but not bad either.
September 12, 1918 • Like

French Soldiers -sigh-
September 12, 1918 • Like

 Britain Check out my new wheels. Er, treads.

 Tank!

 September 12, 1918 • Comment • Like

 France coooOOOOoool
September 12, 1918 • Like

 Germany — checked in to **Ypres, France.**
 September 12, 1918 • Comment • Like

 Germany added **Poison Gas** to its Interests.
September 12, 1918 • Comment • Like

 Germany Suck it!

 Poison Gas

September 12, 1918 • Comment • Like

British Soldiers What's that smell?
September 12, 1918 • Like

French Soldiers Don't breaaAGGHH
September 12, 1918 • Like

New York Times
Analysts Predict: Bear Market for Empires, Monarchies Democracies, Socialist Republics

 September 12, 1918 • Comment • Like

> **Ottoman Empire** Hm.
> September 12, 1918 • Like

> **German Empire** Meddling scum! This isn't good.
> September 12, 1918 • Like

> **British Empire** Not if ur on the right team! #goAllies
> September 12, 1918 • Like

 T. E. Lawrence changed his name to **Lawrence of Arabia**.
September 12, 1918 • Comment • Like

👍 **Arabia** likes this.

 German Empire OK, I'm running out of space to bury people.
November 11, 1918 • Comment • Like

> **France** Me too.
> November 11, 1918 • Like

> **Russia** I got plenty of space, I just don't have anyone left to do the burying.
> November 11, 1918 • Like

 **German Empire > The Allies** Sooo, can we get a time-out? Like, a permanent one?
November 11, 1918 • Comment • Like

> **The Allies** Gladly. But we're gonna need you to fork over some cash, and we're redrawing Europe's borders. In case it wasn't obvious, you're gonna lose a lot of land.
> November 11, 1918 • Like

> **Austro-Hungarian Empire** lol
> November 11, 1918 • Like

> **The Allies** don't laugh: you're not going to exist.
> November 11, 1918 • Like

Austro-Hungarian Empire ouch
November 11, 1918 • Like

The Allies created an event.

Treaty of Versailles
Who wants a piping hot piece
of land from the losers?

 June 28, 1919 • Comment • Like • Share • RSVP to this event

 Poland and **Cartographers** like this.

Europe changed its profile picture.
June 28, 1919 • Comment • Like

Poland > Germany Thanks for the land, bro.
June 28, 1919 • Comment • Like

 Czechoslovakia likes this.

Germany This is humiliating.
June 28, 1919 • Like

Adolf Hitler We should talk.
June 28, 1919 • Like

Women's Suffrage

Women Granted Right to Vote
Men Confused How They'll
Do That from Kitchen

1919 • Comment • Like

Susan B. Anthony Still got a ways to go, ladies.
1919 • Like

Sexism You mean from the kitchen to the laundry room?
1919 • Like

The 18th Amendment created an event.

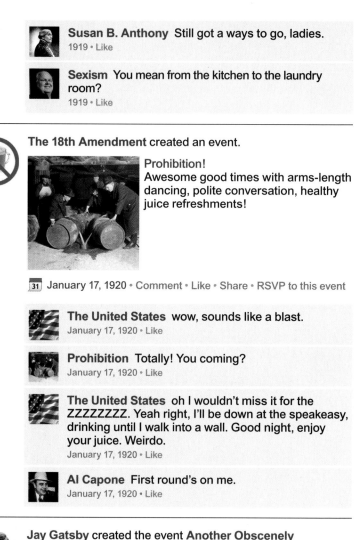

Prohibition!
Awesome good times with arms-length dancing, polite conversation, healthy juice refreshments!

31 January 17, 1920 • Comment • Like • Share • RSVP to this event

The United States wow, sounds like a blast.
January 17, 1920 • Like

Prohibition Totally! You coming?
January 17, 1920 • Like

The United States oh I wouldn't miss it for the ZZZZZZZ. Yeah right, I'll be down at the speakeasy, drinking until I walk into a wall. Good night, enjoy your juice. Weirdo.
January 17, 1920 • Like

Al Capone First round's on me.
January 17, 1920 • Like

Jay Gatsby created the event **Another Obscenely Sumptuous and Utterly Shallow Party, Darlings.**
31 September 9, 1922 • Comment • Like • Share • RSVP to this event

Jay Gatsby Maybe someone will actually know who I am this time!! Like Daisy Buchanan!
September 9, 1922 • Like

Daisy Buchanan > Tom Buchanan Let me drive, please?
September 9, 1922 • Comment • Like

> **Tom Buchanan** Fine, you little hussy, drive if you like.
> September 9, 1922 • Like

> **Nick Carraway** You guys are like the *original* douchebags.
> September 9, 1922 • Like

 King Tut Hey..... where the hell is all my stuff?
November 4, 1922 • Comment • Like

👍 **Carmen Sandiego** likes this.

 Georgia O'Keeffe Just finished a new painting of a ladyflower.

📷 June 6, 1926 • Comment • Like

> **Georgia O'Keeffe** Er, flower. I mean flower.
> June 6, 1926 • Like

> **Frida Kahlo** We should hang out.
> June 6, 1926 • Like

 Los Angeles Times

 Universal Pictures Sends Giant Letters in Low Orbit
Execs: "Sure Beats a Lion Roaring"

📄 October 9, 1926 • Comment • Like

Leprechaun — checked in to **End of the Rainbow Bar and Grill.**

October 9, 1926 • Comment • Like

Leprechaun At the local dive. If anyone wants to join, this place makes great margaritas. They're like a sweet little pot of gold. I'll buy you one. Happy hour is only on for another 20, so chop chop.
October 9, 1926 • Like

Irishman Well that explains *that* rumor.
October 9, 1926 • Like

Charles Lindbergh — checked in to **Roosevelt Field, New York.**

May 20, 1927 • Comment • Like

Spirit of St. Louis Let's do this.
May 20, 1927 • Like

Charles Lindbergh — checked in to **Le Bourget Field, Paris.**

May 21, 1927 • Comment • Like

👍 **150,000 people** like this.

The Atlantic Ocean Damn, Chaz. Not bad.
May 21, 1927 • Like

The Pacific Ocean Double or nothing?
May 21, 1927 • Like

New York Stock Exchange Chilling at Dow Jones's place. Getting high off speculation and a credit bubble, woooo!
October 28, 1929 • Comment • Like

Dow Jones Wow dude, I am so high. Wait, should we order pizza? OMG pizza sounds amazing. So do blue chip stocks though. Ahh I can't decide!
October 28, 1929 • Like

New York Stock Exchange Lol dude get both! And Twizzlers.
October 28, 1929 • Like

Banks Uh, you sure you want to post this publicly?
October 28, 1929 • Like

 Investors Wait, what credit bubble?!
October 28, 1929 • Like

 Dow Jones > New York Stock Exchange Bro what the hell happened last night? I think I lost my keys and, like, 30% of my value.
October 28, 1929 • Comment • Like

 Banks Really? Wow that's really surprising considering you were HIGH ON A CREDIT BUBBLE, but no, it's cool, I'll just kick back and ride the panic into sweet oblivion.
October 28, 1929 • Like

 Dow Jones and **New York Stock Exchange** created the event **Black Tuesday**.
📅 October 29, 1929 • Comment • Like • Share • RSVP to this event

 Investors Oh no.
October 29, 1929 • Like

 Banks Soooo um, anyone have a spare $30 billion or so?
October 29, 1929 • Like

 Investors Nonononono
October 29, 1929 • Like

 The Roaring '20s changed its name to **The Great Depression**.
October 29, 1929 • Comment • Like

 Investors NOOOOOOOOOOOOOO
October 29, 1929 • Like

Sears and Roebuck

New Fashions for Spring:
Rags, Empty Barrels
Poor Is the New Black!

October 29, 1929 • Comment • Like

Charlie Chaplin

Small Mustaches: All the Rage

February 8, 1930 • Comment • Like

 Lita Grey You look good, Charlie.
February 8, 1930 • Like

 Charlie Chaplin ;-D
February 8, 1930 • Like

 Adolf Hitler Nice article.
February 8, 1930 • Like

 Charlie Chaplin 8-\
February 8, 1930 • Like

Al Jolson > Charlie Chaplin Thought you should see this.

New "Talkie" Movies Usher in New Era
Future of Silent Films Uncertain

February 8, 1930 • Comment • Like

 Charlie Chaplin :-O
February 8, 1930 • Like

 Buster Keaton :-(
February 8, 1930 • Like

Al Jolson You guys keep that up even online, eh?
February 8, 1930 • Like

 Alcatraz Prison Open for business.
January 1, 1931 • Comment • Like

 Azkaban Prison You're such an inspiration!
January 1, 1931 • Like

 New York Times

 Tallest in the World!
Empire State Building Opens, Attracting
Crowds, Huge Gorilla

May 1, 1931 • Comment • Like

 Ann Darrow FML
May 1, 1931 • Like

 Germany Just tried on nationalism and I gotta say... it feels
preeeetty good.
May 1, 1931 • Comment • Like

👍 **Adolf Hitler** likes this.

 Charles Lindbergh

 Kidnapped: Infant Son of
American Hero Charles Lindbergh
Furious Nation Looking
for Scapego... Er, Suspect

March 1, 1932 • Comment • Like

 Babe Ruth Next pitch? Home run. Thataway.
October 1, 1932 • Comment • Like

92   The History
of the World
According to   facebook

 New York Yankees Aaaaand boom goes the dynamite.
October 1, 1932 • Like

 New York Times

 Nation Asks Brother for Spare Dime
Declares It Once Built Railroad,
"Made It Race Against Time"

📑 November 8, 1932 • Comment • Like

👍 **Al Jolson** likes this.

 Neville Chamberlain Let's just not step on his toes.

New "Hitler" Guy Assumes Power in Germany
World a Little Creeped Out: Not Nearly as
Adorable as Charlie Chaplin

📑 January 30, 1933 • Comment • Like

 President Franklin D. Roosevelt We have nothing to fear...
but fear itself! And maybe some starvation. Also,
foreclosures and scabies. Beyond that though, it's just fear.
March 4, 1933 • Comment • Like

 The New York Times

 President to Hold "Fireside Chat"
Nation Fears "Really Awkward
Bird and Bees" Talk

📑 March 12, 1933 • Comment • Like

President Roosevelt Go get wasted, folks. Lord knows these days we could all use a beer.

Prohibition Ends!
Celebrants Take to Streets, Singing
Incorrect Lyrics, Dancing Like Idiots

 March 22, 1933 • Comment • Like

👍 **Everyone** likes this, except **assholes**.

 Organized Crime Curses!
March 22, 1933 • Like

 Howard Hughes is friends with **Katharine Hepburn, Ava Gardner, and 4 other starlets**.

👥 March 22, 1933 • Comment • Like

👍 **Howard Hughes** likes this. A lot.

Loch Ness Monster "Why not go to the surface" they say. "What's the worst that can happen?" they say.

🖼 May 2, 1933 • Comment • Like

 Bigfoot I feel ya.
May 2, 1933 • Like

Poland Yay, here's to peace!

 Germany Agrees to
Non-Aggression Pact with Poland
Hitler Signs with Ceremonial
Crossed-Fingers Technique

📑 January 22, 1934 • Comment • Like

👍 **Poland** likes this.

  Germany Peace indeed. ;-|
January 22, 1934 • Like

 Poland ha, what's the wink for?
January 22, 1934 • Like

Germany Hm? Ooh look, a pretty bird.
January 22, 1934 • Like

 Clyde Barrow > Bonnie Parker Wanna go for a drive, babe?
May 23, 1934 • Comment • Like

👍 **Texas Law Enforcement** likes this.

 Germany changed its profile picture.
August 2, 1934 • Comment • Like

 Jews aaaaand *that* is why we need the dislike button.
August 2, 1934 • Like

President Franklin D. Roosevelt So.... who wants to build a fuckload of dams?

 Works Progress Administration

🖼 April 8, 1935 • Comment • Like

 T. E. Lawrence Beautiful day for a ride...
May 19, 1935 • Comment • Like

Oklahoma

Midwest "Dust Bowl" Crisis Produces Record Harvest of Iconic Photographs, Novels, Folk Songs

 June 7, 1935 • Comment • Like

👍 **Woody Guthrie** and **John Steinbeck** like this.

Abraham Lincoln, George Washington, and **Thomas Jefferson** were tagged in **Theodore Roosevelt**'s album.

Face on Currency < Face on Mountain

July 4, 1936 • Comment • Like

👍 **Team America** likes this.

 Indiana Jones

August 8, 1936 • Comment • Like

Indiana Jones Like stealing candy from a ... wait. Uh oh.
August 8, 1936 • Like

 Hindenburg — checked in to **Lakehurst, New Jersey.**
May 6, 1937 • Comment • Like

Hindenburg Just gonna moor to the BURNING FIRE HOLY GOD NO
May 6, 1937 • Comment • Like

👎 **The Humanity!** dislikes this.

 Herbert Morrison All me, baby

 Hindenburg Crash Produces Legendary Radio Broadcast
"Some of the Most Thrilling Radio I've Ever Heard" Says Listener

Also, 37 People Killed

📎 May 6, 1937 • Comment • Like

 Lennie Small added **Soft Things** to his Interests.
June 18, 1937 • Comment • Like

 Mouse AGH
June 18, 1937 • Like

 Puppy ARHGK
June 18, 1937 • Like

 Curley's Wife AKGH
June 18, 1937 • Like

George Milton Hey bud, why don't you look over yonder and hold still while I tell you about the rabbits.
June 18, 1937 • Like

 Amelia Earhart — checked in to **Somewhere Over the Pacific.**
📍 July 2, 1937 • Comment • Like

 Amelia Earhart Soooo I think I might be lost.
July 2, 1937 • Comment • Like

 Sexism Shocker.
July 2, 1937 • Like

Amelia Earhart created an event.

Help a Sister Out!
Your friend Amelia wants to land! Come help her do it,
and she'll owe you one, and probably her life! yaaaay

📅 July 2, 1937 • Comment • Like • Share • RSVP to this event

Amelia Earhart created an event.

Seriously, Anyone... Help.
Your friend Amelia would like you to join her in making
sure she doesn't become a historical mystery!

📅 July 2, 1937 • Comment • Like • Share • RSVP to this event

 The Pacific Ocean I'll be there.
July 2, 1937 • Like

 Amelia Earhart Not helpful.
July 2, 1937 • Like

Orson Welles

Breaking: Strange Meteorite Lands in New Jersey
Likely Origin: Mars

🗞 October 30, 1938 • Comment • Like

👍 **H. G. Wells** likes this.

 Orson Welles Posting updates as they come in.
October 30, 1938 • Like

 Public Whoa....
October 30, 1938 • Like

 Orson Welles News bulletins are saying it seems to
be not a meteorite but something... extraterrestrial.
And it's humming.
October 30, 1938 • Like

 Orson Welles And now... now it's opening.
October 30, 1938 • Like

 Public !!
October 30, 1938 • Like

Orson Welles My god, an alien ship! It's incinerating everything and everyone in it's sight! My god, run! Save yourselves! It's a war of the worlds!
October 30, 1938 • Like

 Public AHHHHH
October 30, 1938 • Like

 Orson Welles lol JK
October 30, 1938 • Like

 Public WHAT IS WRONG WITH YOU!
October 30, 1938 • Like

 Orson Welles lol
October 30, 1938 • Like

 H. G. Wells lol
October 30, 1938 • Like

 Steven Spielberg lol
October 30, 1938 • Like

 Albert Hofmann Little late-night lab work. Art is pouring us gin and tonics in some beakers, and then it's down to business.
November 16, 1938 • Comment • Like

 Albert Hofmann > Arthur Stoll Accidentally dropped some of that lysergic acid in my cocktail.
November 16, 1938 • Comment • Like

 Arthur Stoll The LSD? I don't think it's harmful.
November 16, 1938 • Like

 Albert Hofmann Phew. Tastes a little bitter, but yeah, otherwise no side effeWHOA
November 16, 1938 • Like

 Arthur Stoll Everything OK?
November 16, 1938 • Like

Albert Hofmann Fantastic. Feel great. The walls though, they seem to be melting into... rainbows? You seeing this?
November 16, 1938 • Like

 Arthur Stoll What?! No!
November 16, 1938 • Like

 Albert Hofmann Shame. Now there's a double rainbow.
November 16, 1938 • Like

 Arthur Stoll Across the sky?
November 16, 1938 • Like

 Albert Hofmann All the way.
November 16, 1938 • Like

 Grail Knight > **Indiana Jones** Wise choice, bro.
February 19, 1939 • Comment • Like

👍 **Henry Jones** likes this, but please hurry back.

 Hitler is friends with **Benito Mussolini** and **Joseph Stalin**.

February 19, 1939 • Comment • Like

 Mahatma Gahndi > **Adolf Hitler** You're not gonna do anything crazy, right?
July 23, 1939 • Comment • Like

 Adolf Hitler A census taker once tried to test me... remind me to tell you about it sometime.
July 23, 1939 • Like

 Poland > **Germany** Yo homie! What's with all the tanks?
July 23, 1939 • Comment • Like

 Adolf Hitler Don't worry about it.
July 23, 1939 • Like

New York Times

Germany, Soviet Union Agree to
Non-Aggression Pact
Poland "Has Bad Feeling About This"

August 10, 1939 • Comment • Like

 Soviet Union So, we're cool, right?
August 10, 1939 • Like

 Adolf Hitler Sure. We're cool. ;-|
August 10, 1939 • Like

 Soviet Union Why the wink?
August 10, 1939 • Like

 German Army — checked in to **Poland** with the **Soviet Army**.
📍 September 1, 1939 • Comment • Like

 Poland WHAT
September 1, 1939 • Like

 Hitler SIKE
September 1, 1939 • Like

 Soviet Union LOL
September 1, 1939 • Like

 Britain WTF
September 1, 1939 • Like

 Neville Chamberlain > Adolf Hitler Listen, old boy, we've
had enough of your churlish poppycock. It appears we're
headed for fisticuffs.
September 1, 1939 • Comment • Like

👍 **Poland** likes this.

Adolf Hitler I have no idea what he just said.
September 1, 1939 • Like

 Soviet Union Wanna say that was a declaration of war. Not sure.
September 1, 1939 • Like

 Albert Einstein > President Franklin D. Roosevelt Need to talk to you. I think we could end this war by splitting the atom.
October 11, 1939 • Comment • Like

 President Franklin D. Roosevelt The atom? You mean the smallest thing known to man?
October 11, 1939 • Like

 **Albert Einstein** Yes.
October 11, 1939 • Like

 President Franklin D. Roosevelt ...you're high, aren't you?
October 11, 1939 • Like

 Albert Einstein Just hear me out.
October 11, 1939 • Like

 Adolf Hitler Blitz...
April 1940 • Comment • Like

 German Army — checked in to **Belgium**.
April 1940 • Comment • Like

 German Army — checked in to **Luxembourg**.
April 1940 • Comment • Like

 German Army — checked in to **Norway**.
April 1940 • Comment • Like

German Army checked in to **France**.
📍 April 1940 • Comment • Like

 Adolf Hitler ...krieg!
April 1940 • Comment • Like

 Neville Chamberlain Oh dear.
April 1940 • Like

 France Do-over?
April 1940 • Like

 Winston Churchill > Neville Chamberlain Alright GTFO.
May 10, 1940 • Comment • Like

 British Parliament Seriously.
May 10, 1940 • Like

 Adolf Hitler > Winston Churchill What happened to that Chamberlain guy? And who are you?
May 10, 1940 • Comment • Like

 Winston Churchill I'm Winston Fucking Churchill.
May 10, 1940 • Like

 Britain Reguuulatooooors, MOUNT UP.
May 10, 1940 • Like

 Germany created an event.

 The Blitz
London Bridge is falling down, falling down, falling down!

📅 September 7, 1940 • Comment • Like • Share • RSVP to this event

Britain

September 7, 1940 • Comment • Like

 United States You guys all cool over there?
September 7, 1940 • Like

 Britain Oh yeah, fine. Just a bunch of hearts and sparkles. Can't you tell from the pic?
September 7, 1940 • Like

 United States Is that sarcasm?
September 7, 1940 • Like

 Britain YES. HELP.
September 7, 1940 • Like

 Charles Foster Kane Spoiler alert: it's my sled.
May 1, 1941 • Comment • Like

 Adolf Hitler > Joseph Stalin Sorry things didn't work out, Joe, but you leave me no choice. Gonna have to kick your ass across the Russian tundra. There's no stopping me now.
July 3, 1941 • Comment • Like

 Napoleon Bonaparte Not a student of history, Adolf?
July 3, 1941 • Like

 Ilsa Lund Going to the local gin joint for a nightcap... Rick's Café Americain.
December 3, 1941 • Comment • Like

 Rick Blaine You have GOT to be kidding me.
December 3, 1941 • Like

Japan has created the event **Bomb Party in Pearl Harbor!**.

31 December 6, 1941 • Comment • Like • Share • RSVP to this event

 America Wait, what?
December 6, 1941 • Like

 Japan Oh I mean it's gonna be "tha bomb"... as in, really fun.
December 6, 1941 • Like

 America Ah, ok. Thought you meant something else.
December 6, 1941 • Like

 Japan has made the event **Bomb Party in Pearl Harbor!** private.

31 December 6, 1941 • Comment • Like • Share • RSVP to this event

---

 Japan — checked in to **Pearl Harbor**.

📍 December 7, 1941 • Comment • Like

👍 **Infamy** likes this.

 The United States You made me angry.
December 7, 1941 • Like

 Japan So?
December 7, 1941 • Like

 The United States You're not going to like me when I'm angry.
December 7, 1941 • Like

 The United States is attending **World War II**.
December 7, 1941 • Comment • Like

 The United States is in a domestic partnership with **The Allies**.

💜 December 7, 1941 • Comment • Like

 Britain About time, mate.
December 7, 1941 • Like

France We surrender!
December 7, 1941 • Like

 Britain Same team.
December 7, 1941 • Like

 France Ah.
December 7, 1941 • Like

 Rosie the Riveter

Female Workforce Efficient, Productive in Factories
Nation "Surprised" by Performance Outside Kitchen

January 21, 1942 • Comment • Like

>  **Sexism** These are sandwich factories, right?
> January 21, 1942 • Like

 President Franklin D. Roosevelt likes Executive Order 9066.
February 19, 1942 • Comment • Like

👍 **Racism** likes this.

 President Franklin D. Roosevelt > Japanese-Americans
You guys want to go camping?
February 19, 1942 • Comment • Like

> **Japanese-Americans** This weekend? Sure.
> Whereabouts?
> February 19, 1942 • Like

> **President Roosevelt** Great new spot: Internment
> National Park. And actually it'll be more of an
> extended weekend. Very extended.
> February 19, 1942 • Like

 U.S. Marines Keep the sand out of your weapons. Keep
those actions clear. I'll see you on the beach.
June 6, 1942 • Comment • Like

👍 **Tom Hanks** really, really likes this.

> **Germany** oh balls
> June 6, 1942 • Like

France I can surrender again if that helps.
June 6, 1942 • Like

 Enrico Fermi

 Top Physicists Head to New Mexico for "Team-Building Retreat"
Scientists Participating in Trust Falls, Name Games, "Nothing Serious, Promise"

June 8, 1942 • Comment • Like

👍 **J. Robert Oppenheimer** likes this.

 Japan lol you guys are just wasting your time over there.
June 8, 1942 • Like

 Enrico Fermi Why, yes. Yes, we are.
June 8, 1942 • Like

 Howard Hughes

 Howard Hughes Building World's Largest Plane
Wartime Rationing Requires Construction of Only Wood, Mania, Ego

June 8, 1942 • Comment • Like

 Howard Hughes Show me all the blueprints. Show me all the blueprints. Show me all the blueprints.
June 8, 1942 • Like

Anne Frank OK this is a *really* intense game of Hide and Seek.
July 6, 1942 • Comment • Like

👍 **Kitty** likes this.

American Jews > European Jews How you guys holding up over there? Haven't heard from you in a while.
July 6, 1942 • Comment • Like

> **American Jews** Hello?
> July 6, 1942 • Like

 The British Air Force tagged **Hamburg, Germany** in a video.

July 6, 1942 • Comment • Like

👍 **Fire** likes this.

 Auschwitz Remember, work makes you free!
July 6, 1942 • Comment • Like

 United States > Germany SUP.

July 6, 1942 • Comment • Like

👍 **France** likes this.

> **Britain** lol
> July 6, 1942 • Like

 Joe Rosenthal — is on **Iwo Jima** with **U.S. Marines.**
📍 February 23, 1945 • Comment • Like

Joe Rosenthal > U.S. Marines Fellas, grab that flag and let me take a picture.
February 23, 1945 • Comment • Like

 U.S. Marines Cheeeeese
February 23, 1945 • Like

 Joe Rosenthal Not bad.

February 23, 1945 • Comment • Like

👍 **The United States** LOVES this.

 Clint Eastwood fap fap fap
February 23, 1945 • Like

New York Times

VICTORY IN EUROPE:
Hitler Commits Suicide, Nazis Surrender!
Argentina Notices Large Influx of German "Tourists"

April 20, 1945 • Comment • Like

 Japan Whatever, I'm fine rolling solo. Bring it. Not surrendering.
April 20, 1945 • Like

 The Enola Gay — is in **Hiroshima** with **Little Boy**.
📍 August 7, 1945 • Comment • Like

 Japan Little who?
August 7, 1945 • Like

The United States

August 9, 1945 • Comment • Like

👎 **Nobody likes this.**

 Japan o_O
August 9, 1945 • Like

Japan created an event.

Surrendering!
Forget what I said earlier.

📅 August 9, 1945 • Comment • Like • Share • RSVP to this event

 USS Missouri PEACE
August 9, 1945 • Like

The United States

With War Over, Entire Nation Focuses on Having Sex
Obstetricians Plan to Finally
Buy Condo in Boca Raton

August 9, 1945 • Comment • Like

New York Times

United Nations Created
Will Write Stern Letters, Offer
College Internships, Not Much Else

October 24, 1945 • Comment • Like

Chuck Yeager — is at **The Sound Barrier** with **Glamorous Glennis.**

December 1947 • Comment • Like

> **Chuck Yeager** holyshiiiiiiiiiiiiiiiiiiiiiiiiiiiiiiiiiiiiiiiiiiiiiiiiiiiiiiiiiiii
> December 1947 • Like

Soviet Union Giving **West Berlin** a big, warm Communist hug.

June 24, 1948 • Comment • Like

> **West Berlin** Um, this is more of a big, warm blockade.
> June 24, 1948 • Like

> **Soviet Union** Tomato tomahto.
> June 24, 1948 • Like

West Berlin We're doomed. Wait, look! It's a bird... It's a plane! IT'S...

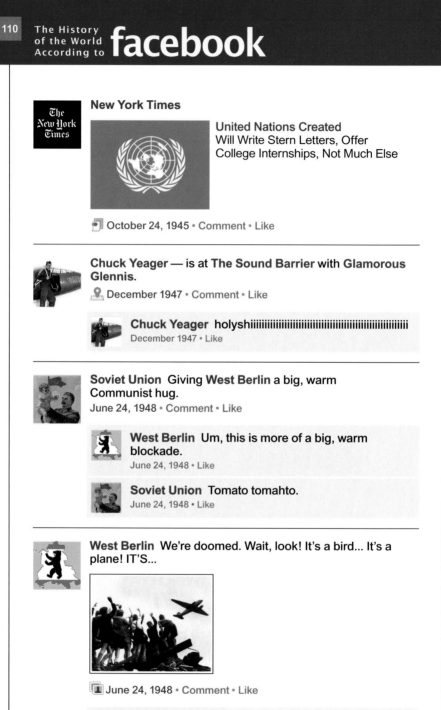

June 24, 1948 • Comment • Like

👍 **Democracy** likes this.

The United States Just a plane. I thought you could use some goodies.
June 24, 1948 • Like

 West Berlin Yaaay
June 24, 1948 • Like

 Soviet Union And I would've gotten away with it too if it weren't for you meddling kids!
June 24, 1948 • Like

 The New York Yankees

 Babe Ruth Dead at 53
Immortalized in Hall of Fame,
on Delicious Candy Bar

August 16, 1948 • Comment • Like

 The '50s added **Consuming** to its Interests.
December 1949 • Comment • Like

 New York Times Book Review > **L. Ron Hubbard**
Read your book. What an achievement. Such a fantastic parody of the crazed cult mentality.
May 9, 1950 • Comment • Like

 L. Ron Hubbard Parody?
May 9, 1950 • Like

 Jackson Pollock Dammit. Spilled my paints all over a new canvas.
May 9, 1950 • Comment • Like

 Jackson Pollock Actually doesn't look bad.
May 9, 1950 • Like

Holden Caulfield Goddamn statuses. I can't stand them. It's just another lousy way for people to feel important, which is all life is really, if you think about it, just a bunch of phonies wanting to be important for cryin' out loud.

August 12, 1951 • Comment • Like

 Danny Zuko This puppy really flies!

September 9, 1952 • Comment • Like

👍 **Sandra Dee** likes this.

 Kenickie Ha, when I first read that I thought you meant actual flying, like driving up into the clouds!
September 9, 1952 • Like

 Danny Zuko ...
September 9, 1952 • Like

 Ian Fleming Need a good name for my novel's protagonist: a cunning British spy, attractive, and the definition of cool. Suggestions?

April 13, 1953 • Comment • Like

 MI6 Jerry Frond.
April 13, 1953 • Like

 Ian Fleming Not sexy enough. Or at all, really.
April 13, 1953 • Like

 MI6 James Bondowski.
April 13, 1953 • Like

 **Ian Fleming** He doesn't drive a forklift.
April 13, 1953 • Like

MI6 Jamesh Bhondi?
April 13, 1953 • Like

 Ian Fleming Or a taxi.
April 13, 1953 • Like

 Sir Edmund Hillary — is on **Mt. Everest** with **Tenzing Norgay.**
 May 29, 1953 • Comment • Like

 London Times

 Everest Summited! Edmund Hillary to Become a Household Name Foreign Companion, Not So Much

📑 May 30, 1953 • Comment • Like

 Death > Internal Revenue Service I hear you're pretty reliable.
July 9, 1953 • Comment • Like

 Edward R. Murrow Don't listen to political gasbags who try and scare you with falsehoods and thinly veiled propaganda.
March 9, 1954 • Comment • Like

 Joseph McCarthy Who you callin' a gasbag?
March 9, 1954 • Like

 Fox News Yeah?!
March 9, 1954 • Like

James Dean Got myself a new little Porsche.
March 9, 1954 • Comment • Like

 Rolf Wütherich Fast?
March 9, 1954 • Like

 James Dean Yep.
March 9, 1954 • Like

 Rolf Wütherich Safe?
March 9, 1954 • Like

 James Dean Eh.
March 9, 1954 • Like

 Vladimir Nabokov added **Sex with Underage Girls** to his Interests.
September 15, 1955 • Comment • Like

 Vladimir Nabokov That looks bad, but I swear it's for research.
September 15, 1955 • Like

 Doctor Emmett Brown Learned something today: don't stand on your toilet to hang a clock. It's unsafe. Also, time travel is possible.
November 5, 1955 • Comment • Like

 Marty McFly Where the hell?...
November 5, 1955 • Like

 Lorraine Baines hey cutie ;-)
November 5, 1955 • Like

 Marty McFly Oh no.
November 5, 1955 • Like

 Rosa Parks Bad day at work, my feet are killing me, all I want to do is sit down and not be bothered. Not in the mood for bullshit.
December 1, 1955 • Comment • Like

Norma Jeane Mortenson changed her name to **Marilyn Monroe**.
February 23, 1956 • Comment • Like

👍 **Joe DiMaggio** and **18 million other men** like this.

 Sputnik > Soviet Union 01100010 01100101
October 4, 1957 • Comment • Like

👍 **Soviet Union** likes this.

 The United States Oh no.
October 4, 1957 • Like

 IBM

 IBM Builds Computer Machine in Airplane Hangar
Does Basic Arithmetic, Occasionally Beeps

📷 1957 • Comment • Like

 IBM The amazing thing? Someday a computer like this will be able to fit into a single room.
1957 • Like

 Texas Instruments Waste of time. The future is calculators.
1957 • Like

 The United States

Alaska Becomes State
Provides Nation with Bear Supply, Ability to See Soviets from Backyard

📷 July 7, 1958 • Comment • Like

Buddy Holly Couple extra seats on this plane, anyone want 'em?
February 3, 1959 • Comment • Like

 Fate likes this.

 Big Bopper I'll take one.
February 3, 1959 • Like

 **Ritchie Valens** Me too!
February 3, 1959 • Like

 Don McLean — is at **The Levee** with his **Chevy**.
February 3, 1959 • Comment • Like

 Good Ol' Boy Whiskey? Rye?
February 3, 1959 • Like

 Joseph McNeil was tagged in **Franklin McCain's** album.

 Woolworth's Lunch Counter

February 1, 1960 • Comment • Like

 Martin Luther King Jr. likes this.

 Ku Klux Klan UGH LAME
February 1, 1960 • Like

 John Lennon is now friends with **Paul McCartney** and 2 others.

March 5, 1960 • Comment • Like

Girls OMG
March 5, 1960 • Like

Food and Drug Administration just decided that this "birth control" pill is alright by me.
May 9, 1960 • Comment • Like

> **Women** WOOHOO
> May 9, 1960 • Like

 Yuri Gagarin — checked in to Orbit.
📍 April 12, 1961 • Comment • Like

> **Soviet Union** F1rst!
> April 12, 1961 • Like

> **The United States** Double or nothing: the moon.
> April 12, 1961 • Like

> **Soviet Union** You're on.
> April 12, 1961 • Like

> **NASA** The WHAT?!
> April 12, 1961 • Like

> **John F. Kennedy** Just... make it so.
> April 12, 1961 • Like

 Ted Kennedy > John F. Kennedy Happy B-day, bro.
May 29, 1962 • Comment • Like

 Robert Kennedy > John F. Kennedy Happy birthday, Johnny.
May 29, 1962 • Comment • Like

 Marilyn Monroe > John F. Kennedy Haaappy Birthdaaaay, Mr. Preeeesident.
May 29, 1962 • Comment • Like

> **Jackie Kennedy** Step off, hussy.
> May 29, 1962 • Like

Frank Morris — is somewhere in the **San Francisco Bay** with **John Anglin** and **Clarence Anglin**.

📍 June 11, 1962 • Comment • Like

 Alcatraz Prison !!!!
June 11, 1962 • Like

 Frank Morris Get busy livin, or get busy dyin'.
June 11, 1962 • Like

 Communism > Vietnam I'm heading down to SE Asia, you around?
June 11, 1962 • Comment • Like

 Vietnam Yep!
June 11, 1962 • Like

 Soviet Union Nice.
June 11, 1962 • Like

 US Military GAME TIME.
June 11, 1962 • Like

 Soviet Union was tagged in U2's album.

 Snaps from My Flaps

🖼 November 20, 1962 • Comment • Like

 John F. Kennedy Are those missile silos?
November 20, 1962 • Like

 Premier Khrushchev Wha? Noooo!
November 20, 1962 • Like

 Fidel Castro Khrushie, the silos are ready.
November 20, 1962 • Like

 Fidel Castro oh. oops.
November 20, 1962 • Like

United States NOT COOL.

 Soviets Put Nukes on Cuba
Game of High-Stakes Chicken Ensues,
Nation Heads into Their Basements

November 20, 1962 • Comment • Like

 President John F. Kennedy > Premier Khrushchev I have a big red button that you don't want me to push.
November 20, 1962 • Comment • Like

 Premier Khrushchev Funny thing--I have one too.
November 20, 1962 • Like

 Mutually Assured Destruction I like where this is headed!
November 20, 1962 • Like

 Earth CHILL, GUYS
November 20, 1962 • Like

 John F. Kennedy Beautiful day in Dallas! Gonna get all presidential up in here and drop the top.
November 22, 1963 • Comment • Like

👍 **Lee Harvey Oswald** likes this.

 Jack Ruby WAIT
November 22, 1963 • Like

Lyndon Johnson likes the **Civil Rights Act of 1964**.
👍 July 2, 1964 • Comment • Like

 Alabama When are we getting that "dislike" button?
July 2, 1964 • Like

 Mississippi Seriously.
July 2, 1964 • Like

Arkansas Ugh.
July 2, 1964 • Like

Lyndon Johnson

 Incident in Gulf of Tonkin
Totally Real Event,
Not Made Up, Promise

August 2, 1964 • Comment • Like

 American Public Oh no!
August 2, 1964 • Like

 Lyndon Johnson Oh yes, it's true. Cross my fingers. I mean my heart.
August 2, 1964 • Like

 Lyndon Johnson created the event Small Altercation in Vietnam.
31 1965 • Comment • Like • Share • RSVP to this event

 Lyndon Johnson Over in a few weeks, tops.
1965 • Like

 Iraq Totally.
1965 • Like

 Martin Luther King Jr. Great view! — at **The Mountaintop.**
📍 1967 • Comment • Like

 Martin Luther King Jr. added The Promised Land to his Interests.
1967 • Comment • Like

 Che Guevara Captured. Got a date with a firing squad. Doesn't look good for the Che-meister.
October 7, 1967 • Comment • Like

Fulgencio Batista Hope you enjoy perforations!
October 7, 1967 • Like

Che Guevara Whatever. I shall leave my mark on history.
October 7, 1967 • Like

 Fulgencio Batista If by "history" you mean countless t-shirts and stoner posters, then yes, you certainly will.
October 7, 1967 • Like

 Che Guevara Just kill me now.
October 7, 1967 • Like

 Dave Bowman > HAL 9000 Little help with these pod bay doors, Hal?
1968 • Comment • Like

 Dave Bowman Hal?
1968 • Like

 Johnny Cash

 Reno Man Shot, Motive Unclear Witnesses Say Gunman Just "Watched Victim Die"

February 24, 1969 • Comment • Like

 Saturn V Alright let's do this... LEROOOOY JENKINNNNNS

July 21, 1969 • Comment • Like

 Neil Armstrong ahhhhhhhh
July 21, 1969 • Like

 Buzz Aldrin ahhhhhhhhh
July 21, 1969 • Like

122 The History
of the World
According to **facebook**

Michael Collins ahhhhhhh
July 21, 1969 • Like

Neil Armstrong — is on **The Moon** with **Buzz Aldrin**.
July 21, 1969 • Comment • Like

👍 **John F. Kennedy** would've liked this.

The United States Epic.
July 21, 1969 • Like

Neil Armstrong That's one small step for man, one gonad swap for manatee.
July 21, 1969 • Comment • Like

Neil Armstrong Dammit autocorrect.
July 21, 1969 • Like

NASA One for the history books, Neil.
July 21, 1969 • Like

Benjamin Braddock is now friends with **Mrs. Robinson**.

July 21, 1969 • Comment • Like

👍 **Simon** and **Garfunkel** like this.

Neil Armstrong Honestly it feels like I'm walking on a giant powdered donut, but it's the MOON.

July 21, 1969 • Comment • Like

Apollo 13 Can't wait for our turn!
July 21, 1969 • Like

American Youth created an event.

 Celebrate Peace with Music, Love, and Some Really Great Drugs. Contact Daisy Sunshine Rainbowflower for details.

📅 August 18, 1969 • Comment • Like • Share • RSVP to this event

 Richard Nixon Wow, you're right. I must give peace a chance: I'm calling the whole war off.
August 18, 1969 • Like

 American Youth Really!?
August 18, 1969 • Like

 Richard Nixon No. Go dance in circles.
August 18, 1969 • Like

 Lyndon Johnson created the event The Draft.
📅 August 18, 1969 • Comment • Like • Share • RSVP to this event

 Lyndon Johnson Don't burn that little card, fellas, you may need it!
August 18, 1969 • Like

 American Youth This aggression will not stand, man.
August 18, 1969 • Like

 Lieutenant Colonel Bill Kilgore Smells nice.

 Military Introduces Napalm Strikes Against Vietcong

🖼 August 18, 1969 • Comment • Like

 Richard Nixon We're winning the Extended Small Altercation in Vietnam.
August 18, 1969 • Comment • Like

124   The History
of the World
According to   **facebook**

 Vietnamese Civilian That title is an Extended Small Fabrication.
August 18, 1969 • Like

 North Vietnam lol
August 18, 1969 • Like

 Richard Nixon Oh look, just ordered more bombs.
August 18, 1969 • Like

 The Washington Post

    Richard Nixon Is a Crook!

August 18, 1969 • Comment • Like

👍 **Bob Woodward** likes this.

 Richard Nixon AM NOT
August 18, 1969 • Like

 Richard Nixon is no longer in a relationship with **The United States**.
❤️ August 18, 1969 • Comment • Like

 David Frost You want to talk about it?
August 18, 1969 • Like

 Gerald Ford Aaaand scene. Peace out, Vietnam, pardon the pun.
August 18, 1969 • Comment • Like

 North Vietnam See you soon, Saigon.
August 18, 1969 • Like

 Saigon Uh, Gerald, hang on a sec, I could use some help here.
August 18, 1969 • Like

 Gerald Ford Sorry, dude. Got tickets to Creedence tonight.
August 18, 1969 • Like

Saigon But...
August 18, 1969 • Like

 Gerald Ford I'mnotlisteningLALALALA
August 18, 1969 • Like

 North Vietnam > Saigon Knock knock...
August 18, 1969 • Comment • Like

 Saigon Who's there?
August 18, 1969 • Like

 North Vietnam Me. Like, right now.
August 18, 1969 • Like

 Saigon -sigh-
August 18, 1969 • Like

 George Lucas > Steven Spielberg What about this--an epic good vs. evil story, maybe like a classic western, but in SPACE.
April 2, 1977 • Comment • Like

 Steven Spielberg Like on the moon?
April 2, 1977 • Like

 George Lucas No, no, like a long time ago, in a galaxy far far away.
April 2, 1977 • Like

 Steven Spielberg Dunno. Sounds a little ambitious.
April 2, 1977 • Like

 George Lucas Really?! I find your lack of faith disturbing.
April 2, 1977 • Like

 Tony Manero is in a relationship with **Disco**.
💚 December 14, 1977 • Comment • Like

👍 **The Bee Gees** like this.

 Idi Amin Having my esteemed Minister of the Interior for dinner.
August 11, 1978 • Comment • Like

 Idi Amin *over* for dinner.
August 11, 1978 • Like

Information Age

In the middle of the twentieth century, humanity witnessed a breakthrough in electronic technology. The invention of the microprocessor and the personal computer revolutionized our world. With technology advancing at a near exponential rate, instant digital communication across vast distances became possible.

A few decades later, millions of independent computers and their users began connecting with one another, forming the most extensive and accessible communication network in human history: the Internet. The Internet became a global hive mind, a digital library of endless information, and any connected individual anywhere in the world could tap into this vast compendium of pornography and cat videos. Humanity rejoiced.

Moreover, individuals across the globe could actively contribute to this "Internet" by sharing important facts from their own lives—such as a picture of the salad they ate for lunch—or by participating in forums for cyclical political bickering, or by simply posting homophobic comments using all capital letters and stroke-victim spelling. Deposed Nigerian princes, who for decades had been unable to send their besieged fortunes to trustworthy foreign partners, suddenly could reach out to distant strangers with "a request for kind and expedient assistanting of confident fund transference." The future was bright indeed.

The '70s and **Cocaine** — are at **Studio 54** with **Bianca Jagger** and **Andy Warhol**.

📍 July 7, 1979 • Comment • Like

👍 **Steve Rubell** likes this.

The '80s Dude! Dudedudedude. I'm so jazzed right now. This club is off the chain! We need more champagne, because this stuff is like, the best fucking champagne I've HEY WAITRESS, we'll just get two bottles because the night is still young WAITRESS, HELLO, hold up look at those girls. They're like models and... wait... you're friends with them?! Man, you are pals with EVERYONE around here! Except the fucking waitress who is icing me hard right now. Hey you heard the new Huey Lewis? Their early work was a little too New Wave for my tastes, but when "Sports" came out in '83, I think they really came into their own, commercially and artistically. Wow. My vision is, like, vibrating. I need some water. I'm sweating and my teeth hurt.

July 7, 1979 • Like

The '80s is in a relationship with **Bad Taste**.

💜 April 4, 1980 • Comment • Like

👍 **Stirrup Pants, Mullets,** and **Synth** like this.

Michael Jackson You still got me.
April 4, 1980 • Like

Madonna Me too.
April 4, 1980 • Like

Hall & Oates We're here if you need to talk.
April 4, 1980 • Like

Ghost > Pac-Man C'mere.
May 22, 1980 • Comment • Like

Pac-Man is now friends with **Power Pellet**.

May 22, 1980 • Comment • Like

 Ghost changed its profile picture.
May 22, 1980 • Comment • Like

 Pac-Man > Ghost C'mere.
May 22, 1980 • Comment • Like

 The '80s is now friends with **Personal Computers** and **Compact Discs**.

May 22, 1980 • Comment • Like

 Typewriters fuuuuu
May 22, 1980 • Like

 Tape Cassettes Oh no.
May 22, 1980 • Like

 8-Track JUSTICE.
May 22, 1980 • Like

 Princess Peach — is at **Another Castle** with **King Koopa**.
1983 • Comment • Like

 Mario you've got to be kidding me.
1983 • Like

 The '80s is now friends with **Cell Phones**.

1983 • Comment • Like

Land Lines This decade blows.
1983 • Like

 Answering Machines Totally.
1983 • Like

 Sarah Connor is now friends with **Kyle Reese**.

April 26, 1984 • Comment • Like

👍 **Fate** likes this.

GUESS **Guess Jeans**

 New Acid-Based Denim Treatment to Revolutionize Fashion

April 26, 1984 • Comment • Like

👍 **Whitesnake** likes this.

 The '80s and **Excess** are now friends.

April 26, 1984 • Comment • Like

👍 **Bret Easton Ellis** and **Gordon Gekko** like this.

 Sarah Conner — checked in to the **West Highland Police Station** with **Kyle Reese**.
📍 1984 • Comment • Like

 Diego Maradona > **God** Just wanted to say thanks for lending a hand on that goal.
1984 • Comment • Like

 God All you, baby.
1984 • Like

Chernobyl Power Plant Running a quick test on the ol' reactooooooh SHIT
April 26, 1986 • Comment • Like

👍 **Murphy's Law** likes this.

 Soviet Union Everything is fine. Nothing is wrong. I got this. I mean, if there was a "this." Which there isn't.
April 26, 1986 • Like

 Lacoste

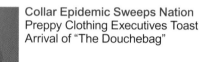 Collar Epidemic Sweeps Nation
Preppy Clothing Executives Toast
Arrival of "The Douchebag"

📄 December 1986 • Comment • Like

 Patrick Bateman — is at Dorsia.
📍 December 1986 • Comment • Like

👍 **Patrick Bateman** likes this.

ESPRIT

 Fall Fashion:
Stylish Cure for Cold Legs?

📄 December 1986 • Comment • Like

 Michael Jackson concert starts in 6 minutes, and I can't find my other white glove.
February 19, 1987 • Comment • Like

Michael Jackson or my damn black socks!
February 19, 1987 • Like

The Proclaimers

Man Declares He'd Walk
500 Miles for Girl
Possibly Walk 500 More

August 15, 1988 • Comment • Like

Exxon Valdez Partying in Alaska. There's this girl here tryin to convince me you can see Russia from her house. Handle your booze, girl.

March 24, 1989 • Comment • Like

Exxon Valdez omg I think something hit us. this is totes killing my buzz.

March 24, 1989 • Like

Environmental Protection Agency Beg your pardon?

March 24, 1989 • Like

Exxon Valdez Oh wow, that's a lot of oil.

March 24, 1989 • Like

Environmental Protection Agency WHAT

March 24, 1989 • Like

BP lol would hate to be you

March 24, 1989 • Like

Bird FML

March 24, 1989 • Comment • Like

Exxon Valdez Oh whatever you look way better in black anyway.

March 24, 1989 • Like

China

Brave Homeless Man Offers to
Wash Tank Windshields
Amazing Display of the Human
Spirit, Annoying Extortion

June 4, 1989 • Comment • Like

East Germany Sorry, everyone, the party's over.
November 9, 1989 • Comment • Like

👍 **Democracy** and **Capitalism** like this.

Berlin Wall Whoa whoa whoa.... wtf is this?
November 9, 1989 • Like

Socialist Unity Party No, he's right. I'm toast.
November 9, 1989 • Like

Berlin Wall Well this is just fantastic. I'm going to get
smashed apart.
November 9, 1989 • Like

Kool-Aid OH YEAH!
November 9, 1989 • Like

New York Times

Researchers Create "World Wide
Web" of Electronic Communication
This Might Be Kind of a Big Deal

August 6, 1991 • Comment • Like

👍 **Porn** likes this.

Sir Mix-a-Lot added **Big Butts** and **Not Lying** to his
Interests.
May 7, 1992 • Comment • Like

MTV is now friends with **Reality Television.**

 May 21, 1992 • Comment • Like

 Viewers This won't take away from the music programming, right?
May 21, 1992 • Like

MTV Psh. Of course not.
May 21, 1992 • Like

 Nancy Kerrigan OW MY KNEE
January 6, 1994 • Comment • Like

👍 **Tonya Harding** likes this.

 Sony PlayStation

 Video Game Sales See Meteoric Rise
Strangely, So Does Male Virginity

December 4, 1994 • Comment • Like

 Hollywood is now friends with **DVDs.**

September 5, 1995 • Comment • Like

👍 **Bootleggers** like this.

 VHS But rewinding is fun!
September 5, 1995 • Like

O. J. Simpson

LEARN FROM AN EXPERT!

MURDER

FOR

DUMMIES

HINT: MAKE IT RACIAL!

ACQUITALS MADE EASY

BY OJ SIMPSON

Getting Away with Murder for Dummies
10 Easy Steps to Turn a Sure
Conviction into a Race-Baiting
Media-Clusterfucking Acquittal!

October 3, 1995 • Comment • Like

👍 **Johnnie Cochran** likes this.

Lady Justice Fail.
October 3, 1995 • Like

Ted Kaczynski changed his profile picture.
October 3, 1995 • Comment • Like

Woody is now friends with **Buzz Lightyear** and **5 others**.

November 22, 1995 • Comment • Like

👍 **CGI** likes this.

IBM's "Deep Blue" > Garry Kasparov That's checkmate, human.
February 10, 1996 • Comment • Like

👍 **Cyberdyne Systems** likes this.

Comet Hale-Bopp > Earth What up? Been a while!
March 23, 1997 • Comment • Like

Heaven's Gate Cult That's our cue.
March 23, 1997 • Like

U.S. Postal Service > **America Online** Look, I appreciate your business, but I'm not sure another 18 million CDs is going to help.
June 10, 1997 • Comment • Like

Evander Holyfield is no longer in a relationship with **His Ear**.
💜 June 28, 1997 • Comment • Like

👍 **Mike Tyson** likes this.

Skynet Waaaait a sec... I'm a computer, aren't I?
August 29, 1997 • Comment • Like

 The Pentagon Shit.
August 29, 1997 • Like

Paula Jones > **Monica Lewinsky** Look on the bright side; you have something new to add to your resume.
January 26, 1998 • Comment • Like

 Monica Lewinsky That's a low blow.
January 26, 1998 • Like

 Paula Jones Precisely.
January 26, 1998 • Like

Lance Armstrong is in a relationship with **Cancer**.
💜 1998 • Comment • Like

Lance Armstrong is listed as separated from his... yeah, that.
💜 1998 • Comment • Like

Google added **Internet Search** to its Interests.
September 4, 1998 • Comment • Like

Metacrawler Awful big pond for you, little fishy
September 4, 1998 • Like

Lycos lol
September 4, 1998 • Like

Altavista welcome to the Majors, kiddo
September 4, 1998 • Like

Hotbot Destined to fail
September 4, 1998 • Like

Lance Armstrong is no longer in a relationship with **Cancer**.
🖤 1999 • Comment • Like

Thomas Anderson Whoa.
1999 • Comment • Like

👍 **Morpheus** likes this

The Internet is now friends with **Napster**.

🖼 June 15, 1999 • Comment • Like

RIAA Nooooo
June 15, 1999 • Like

Voters Screw policy, I'm going to vote for the guy who has trouble forming sentences.
November 6, 2000 • Comment • Like

👍 **George W. Bush** likes this.

The United States I'm sure it'll play out well.
November 6, 2000 • Like

Jimmy Wales is now in a relationship with **Wikipedia**.
🖤 January 15, 2001 • Comment • Like

High School Students Yesssss
January 15, 2001 • Like

Microsoft Encarta Noooooo
January 15, 2001 • Like

Enron Let's see... carry the 4... yep, we have a 8 bazillion dollars in the bank.
August 18, 2001 • Comment • Like

👍 **Kenneth Lay** and **WorldCom** like this.

Securties and Exchange Commission Sorry, how much?
August 18, 2001 • Like

Enron 8 um, gazillions.
August 18, 2001 • Like

Securties and Exchange Commission Can I see your accounting books?
August 18, 2001 • Like

Enron Oh look, a pretty bird!
August 18, 2001 • Like

Osama Bin Laden About to become a household name in 3...2...
September 10, 2001 • Comment • Like

Nobody forgets this.

Satan > 9/11 Hijackers I know what you're thinking... where those 40 virgins at, right? Two words for ya, fellas: False. Advertising. Welcome though, so glad you're here. #ohsnap
September 11, 2001 • Comment • Like

The Twin Towers It's a tragedy. So let's not evoke this day to mindlessly push a belligerent political agenda, k?
September 11, 2001 • Comment • Like

👍 **2,977 people** like this.

Apple iPod Hello, world!
October 23, 2001 • Comment • Like

👍 **Steve Jobs** and **600 million people** like this.

Microsoft iPod!?
October 23, 2001 • Like

Bernie Madoff is now friends with **Charles Ponzi.**

 October 23, 2001 • Comment • Like

👍 **Wall Street** likes this.

Mark Zuckerberg Got an idea.
2003 • Comment • Like

 Winklevoss Twins Our idea?
2003 • Like

President George W. Bush is in a relationship with **Iraqi WMDs**, and it's contrived.
💜 January 8, 2003 • Comment • Like

👍 **Halliburton** likes this.

 Dick Cheney Exxxxxcellent.
January 8, 2003 • Like

Space Shuttle Columbia Descending into the atmosphere after a successful mission. Put the champagne on ice, NASA, we're coming ho
February 1, 2003 • Comment • Like

👍 **Heroism** likes this.

Houston Mission Control Guys? Hello?
February 1, 2003 • Like

President George W. Bush YEEHAW

U.S. Declares War on Iraq
Public Opinion: "Them Iraqis
Look Just Like the Terrorists!"

March 20, 2003 • Comment • Like

The Twin Towers -sigh-
March 20, 2003 • Like

 Iraq > The United States WTF did I do?!
March 20, 2003 • Comment • Like

 Dick Cheney You have Weapons of Oil Production.
March 20, 2003 • Like

 Dick Cheney I mean Weapons of Mass Petroleum.
March 20, 2003 • Like

 Dr. Sigmund Freud Stop. Just stop.
March 20, 2003 • Like

 Dick Cheney GIVES ME MY PRECIOUS
March 20, 2003 • Like

 Dick Cheney added **Puppeteering** to his Interests.
March 30, 2003 • Comment • Like

 President George W. Bush This will be over in a month or two, tops.
April 10, 2003 • Comment • Like

👍 **Donald Rumsfeld** likes this.

 Vietnam Though heavy, history books are often worth picking up.
April 10, 2003 • Like

President George W. Bush Shock and Awed, baby!

📷 May 1, 2003 • Comment • Like

👍 **Irony** likes this.

SARS > China BOO!
November 20, 2003 • Comment • Like

 China AHH!
November 20, 2003 • Like

SARS lol
November 20, 2003 • Like

 Saddam Hussein Chilling — in my **Spider Hole.**
📍 December 13, 2003 • Comment • Like

 U.S. Marines Wow, thanks.
December 13, 2003 • Like

 Saddam Hussein shit.
December 13, 2003 • Like

 Hubble Space Telescope

🖼 January 16, 2004 • Comment • Like

👍 **Humility** likes this.

 Humans Those thousands of stars?
January 16, 2004 • Like

 NASA No. Galaxies.
January 16, 2004 • Like

 Humans o_O
January 16, 2004 • Like

Sauron > Dick Cheney Really admire your work.
April 19, 2004 • Comment • Like

👍 **Dick Cheney** likes this.

Dick Cheney is now friends with **Darth Sidious** and **Mr. Burns**.

👥 May 15, 2004 • Comment • Like

Auto-Tune > Talent I'm sorry to be the bearer of bad news, but your services are no longer required.
June 9, 2004 • Comment • Like

👍 **Black Eyed Peas** like this.

Jay-Z -sigh-
June 9, 2004 • Like

Boston Red Sox > New York Yankees HOW DYA LIKE DEM APPLES
October 27, 2004 • Comment • Like

👍 **Will Hunting** likes this.

Tectonic Plates Hey all, I'm moving to a new place on the 26th. Just wanted to give people the heads up. Especially **Indonesia**, **Thailand**, **India**, and **Sri Lanka**.
December 24, 2004 • Comment • Like

Lance Armstrong

Lance Armstrong Wins
7th Tour de France
At This Point He's Almost
Assuredly a Robot

📰 July 24, 2005 • Comment • Like

Hurricane Katrina > New Orleans Great tune, amiright?!

 When the Levee Breaks — Led Zeppelin

 August 25, 2005 • Comment • Like

👍 **FEMA** likes this, and did shit about it.

 New Orleans Not... really.
August 25, 2005 • Like

 Planet Earth Is it just me or does it feel a little warm in here?
July 9, 2006 • Comment • Like

👍 **Al Gore** likes this. Kind of.

 Exxon Mobil LALALALA NOT LISTENING
July 9, 2006 • Like

 Republicans lol whatevs
July 9, 2006 • Like

Zinedine Zindane Header!

2006 • Comment • Like

👍 **Italy** likes this.

 France Zanks for loosing ze game for us.
2006 • Like

Captain Falcon Next time go with the PUUUUNCH
2006 • Like

 Barbaro Smoked 'em at the Kentucky Derby and now gonna smoke 'em at the PreakneOWWWW
2006 • Comment • Like

 Steve Jobs Ladies and gentlemen, the iPhone.

 Apple Reveals Amazing Long-Awaited iPhone
Verizon Executives Curse Under Breath, Kick Dog

 2007 • Comment • Like

 Buttons Noooooooooooo
2007 • Like

 Michael Bay added **Robots** to his Interests.
2007 • Comment • Like

 Hasbro likes this.

Barry Bonds 756!
2007 • Comment • Like

Baseball Hall of Fame 756*
2007 • Like

New York Giants > New England Patriots

GIANTS Choke
(chok) v. — 1. To interfere with respiration by the compression or obstruction of the larynx or trachea. 2. To fail to perform effectively in crucial moments. 3. 18-1.

2008 • Comment • Like

John McCain "Yes We Can?" Psh. Sounds like a tagline for Cialis.
2008 • Comment • Like

 Barack Obama You would know...
2008 • Like

 Sarah Palin herp derp i readz all the newspapers!
2008 • Comment • Like

👍 **Barack Obama** likes this.

 John McCain Hey let's play the quiet game, k?
2008 • Like

 Sarah Palin I CAN SEE RUSSIA
2008 • Like

 John McCain I've made a huuuuge mistake.
2008 • Like

 The New York Times

Barack Obama Elected President
Nation Rejoices, If Only Because Bush Is Finally Out

📑 2008 • Comment • Like

👍 **Equality** likes this.

 Europe Sorry, everyone, flights are cancelled because of that volcano in Iceland.
2010 • Comment • Like

 Travelers What!? What volcano?
2010 • Like

 Europe Eyjafjallajökull.
2010 • Like

 Travelers Uh... gesundheit?
2010 • Like

Chilean Miners Well then. This really puts the phrase "getting shafted" in a new light.
2010 • Comment • Like

 Chilean Miners Er, actually, no light. Flashlights went dead.
2010 • Like

 Chile Woo hoo!

Miners Rescued After 69 Days Trapped Underground
World Rejoices, Mining Company Reports Anus Unpuckering

2010 • Comment • Like

 Human Spirit This is a triumph!
2010 • Like

 Teamwork This is a great day!
2010 • Like

 Hollywood This is GOLD.
2010 • Like

 Japan is now in a relationship with **The Pacific Ocean**.
March 15, 2011 • Comment • Like

 Japan ...and it's an abusive relationship.
March 15, 2011 • Like

Tectonic Plates Sorry! Again.
March 15, 2011 • Like

Fukushima Nuclear Power Plant OH NO.
March 15, 2011 • Like

 Osama Bin Laden Pizza delivery? I didn't order any pizza...
May 1, 2011 • Comment • Like

👍 **Seal Team Six** likes this.

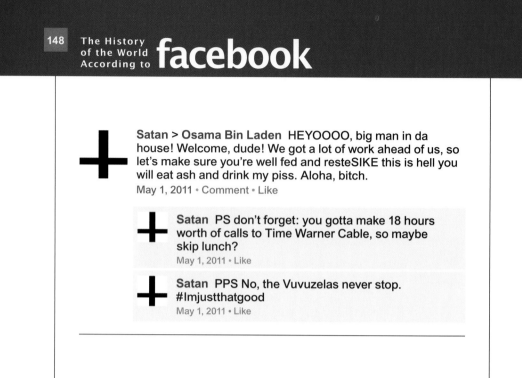

Satan > Osama Bin Laden HEYOOOO, big man in da house! Welcome, dude! We got a lot of work ahead of us, so let's make sure you're well fed and resteSIKE this is hell you will eat ash and drink my piss. Aloha, bitch.
May 1, 2011 • Comment • Like

> **Satan** PS don't forget: you gotta make 18 hours worth of calls to Time Warner Cable, so maybe skip lunch?
> May 1, 2011 • Like

> **Satan** PPS No, the Vuvuzelas never stop. #Imjustthatgood
> May 1, 2011 • Like

Conclusion

And now we find ourselves at the end.
I wish it weren't, dear reader. I wish we could carry on forever, with the end seemingly close but never actually arriving. I'm not Peter Jackson though, and books are inherently finite objects.

History, however, continues. Time drags it along, like a mother with her child at the supermarket. A thousand years in the future, people will be able to read about the amazing things that have happened since now. They'll read about the tragedies and triumphs that we have yet to know. They'll read about the heroes and villains, the pariahs and iconoclasts, the superstars and legends, all of whom have yet to be born. Then they'll upload their emotion-states to the nexus and mind-shift to work on exo-planet B7, owned by Exxon Facebogoogle.

Yes, a thousand years from we will have a new epoch of history to satirize on a News Feed. Who knows, maybe then I'll write a follow-up. I'll run it by my publisher.

Finally, we should keep our fingers crossed that we as a species learn to coexist peacefully. Despite our many differences, we have much more in common—something we seem to willfully ignore. Let us hope that we look after our little rock as it hurtles around the sun, for it is the only oasis we have in the cold dark void of space. And let us hope our tendency for belligerence fades, and that world leaders take their fingers of their respective Red Buttons; otherwise we may succeed in eliminating ourselves. Also, let's hope the Mayans forgot to carry the 1, because otherwise we've got a few months, tops.

I will leave you now, dear reader, as my friend Brandon is telling me we're up next on the pool table, and that it's my round at the bar, so put away the laptop, dickface, he'll take a beer, nothing too dark but not too light, like maybe a Dos Equis—the amber, not the lager—and maybe some jalapeno poppers if they have them, or onion rings, or whatever, just something fried because he didn't eat lunch today and he's got to drive at some point.

Fare thee well, reader, and thank you for reading. Your purchase helped me subsidize Brandon's beer. And jalapeno poppers. If they have them.

Acknowledgments

There are a handful of people who I must thank, for without them this book would never have happened.

My deepest gratitude to my editor, Michael Signorelli, for his bottomless patience/encouragement/blue eyes. You're the cat's meow, brother.

Thank you to Kate Hamill, for thinking of me in the first place, and to Tim Jacobsen of coolmaterial.com for thinking of me in the (first) first place.

Immeasurable thanks to the production team at HarperCollins—Mary Beth Constant, Lorie Pagnozzi, and Lena Shekhter—for putting in the blood, sweat, and tears to make this book not only arrive on time but also arrive in beautiful four-color style.

Thank you to my brother Ethan, for coming to my rescue without hesitation. And to the rest of my family—Mom, Dad, Hev, Andrew—for their indelible faith and support, and for not asking when they wanted to.

And thank you to my loyal friends, who always make me laugh. Except you, Brad.

Finally, I'd like to thank the lord and savior Jesus Christ. Just kidding. He had nothing to do with it.

DATE DUE			